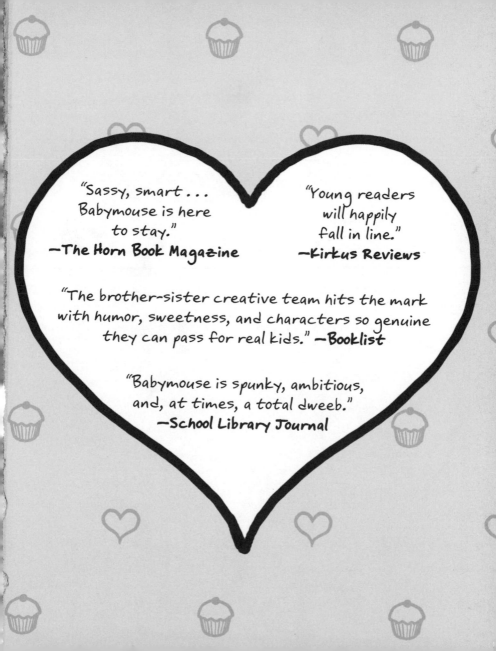

"Sassy, smart . . . Babymouse is here to stay."
—The Horn Book Magazine

"Young readers will happily fall in line."
—Kirkus Reviews

"The brother-sister creative team hits the mark with humor, sweetness, and characters so genuine they can pass for real kids." —Booklist

"Babymouse is spunky, ambitious, and, at times, a total dweeb."
—School Library Journal

Be sure to read **all** the **BABYMOUSE** books:

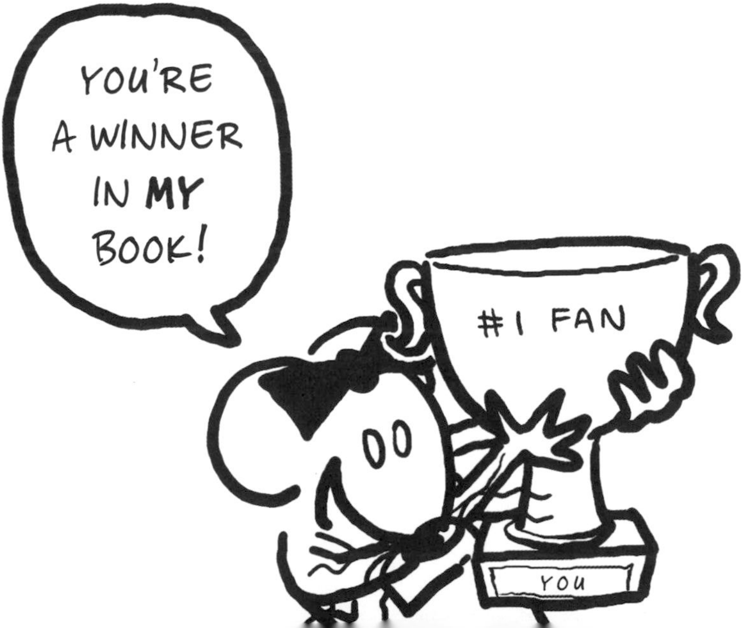
YOU'RE A WINNER IN **MY** BOOK!
#1 FAN
YOU

BABYMOUSE
SKATER GIRL

BY JENNIFER L. HOLM & MATTHEW HOLM

RANDOM HOUSE 🏠 NEW YORK

YOU'D THINK THEY COULD COME UP WITH SOMETHING MORE INTERESTING TO PUT ON THIS PAGE.

Published in the United States by Random House Children's Books, a division of Random House, Inc., New York.

SBCEPNIPVTF and colophon are registered trademarks of Random House, Inc.

www.randomhouse.com/kids
www.babymouse.com

Educators and librarians, for a variety of teaching tools, visit us at
www.randomhouse.com/teachers

Library of Congress Cataloging-in-Publication Data
Holm, Jennifer L.
Babymouse : skater girl / Jennifer L. Holm & Matthew Holm.
   p.   cm.
ISBN 978-0-375-83989-4 (trade) — ISBN 978-0-375-93989-1 (lib. bdg.)
1. Graphic novels. I. Holm, Matthew. II. Title. III. Title: Skater girl.
PN6727.H592 B35 2007 741.5'973—dc22 2006050444

MANUFACTURED IN MALAYSIA

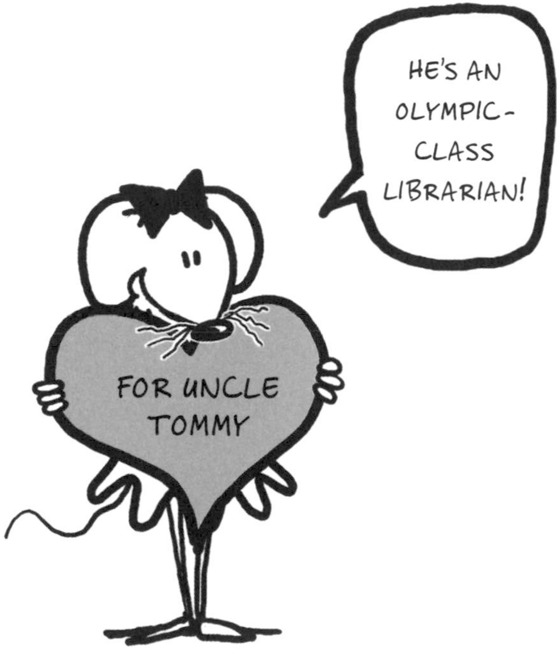
HE'S AN OLYMPIC-CLASS LIBRARIAN!
FOR UNCLE TOMMY

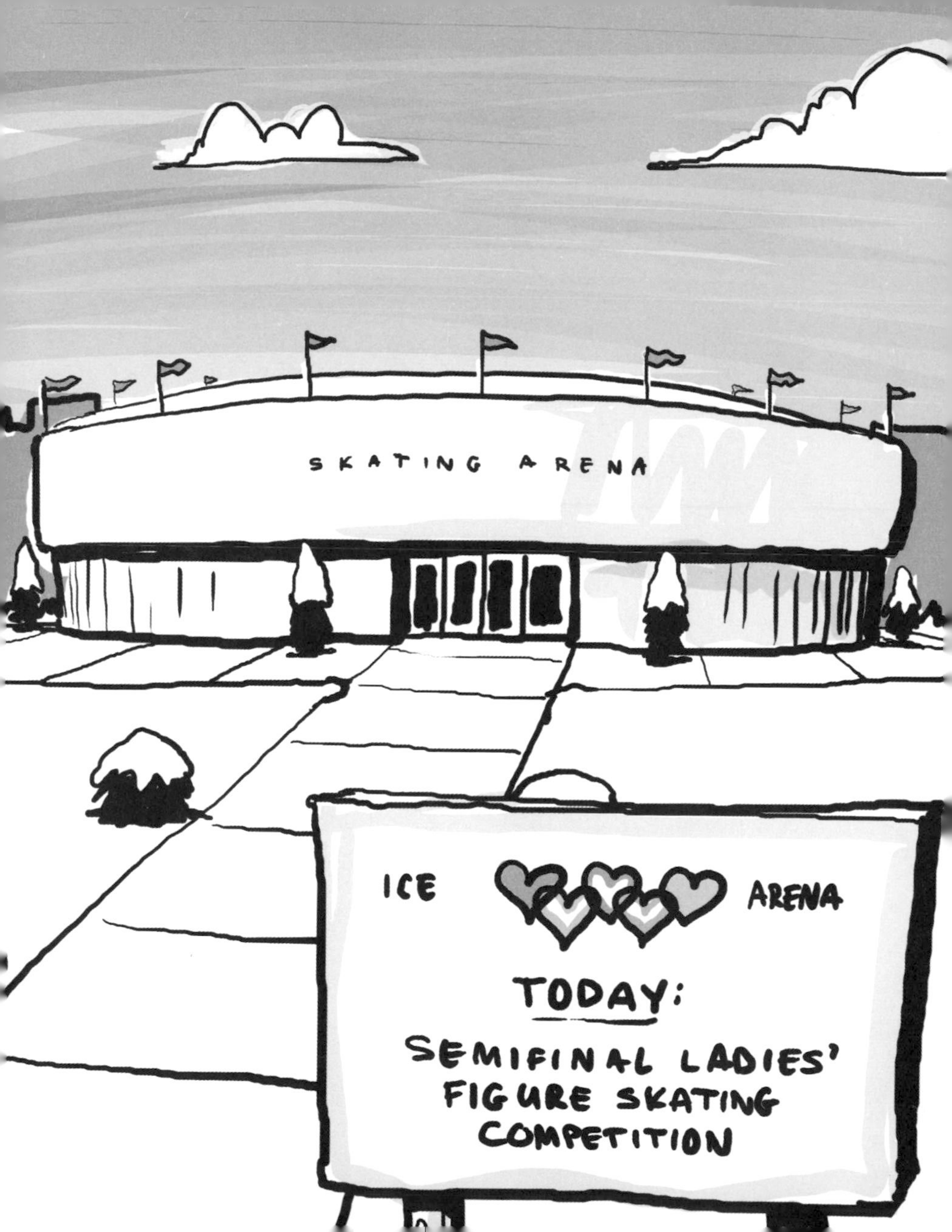
SKATING ARENA
ICE ARENA
TODAY:
SEMIFINAL LADIES' FIGURE SKATING COMPETITION

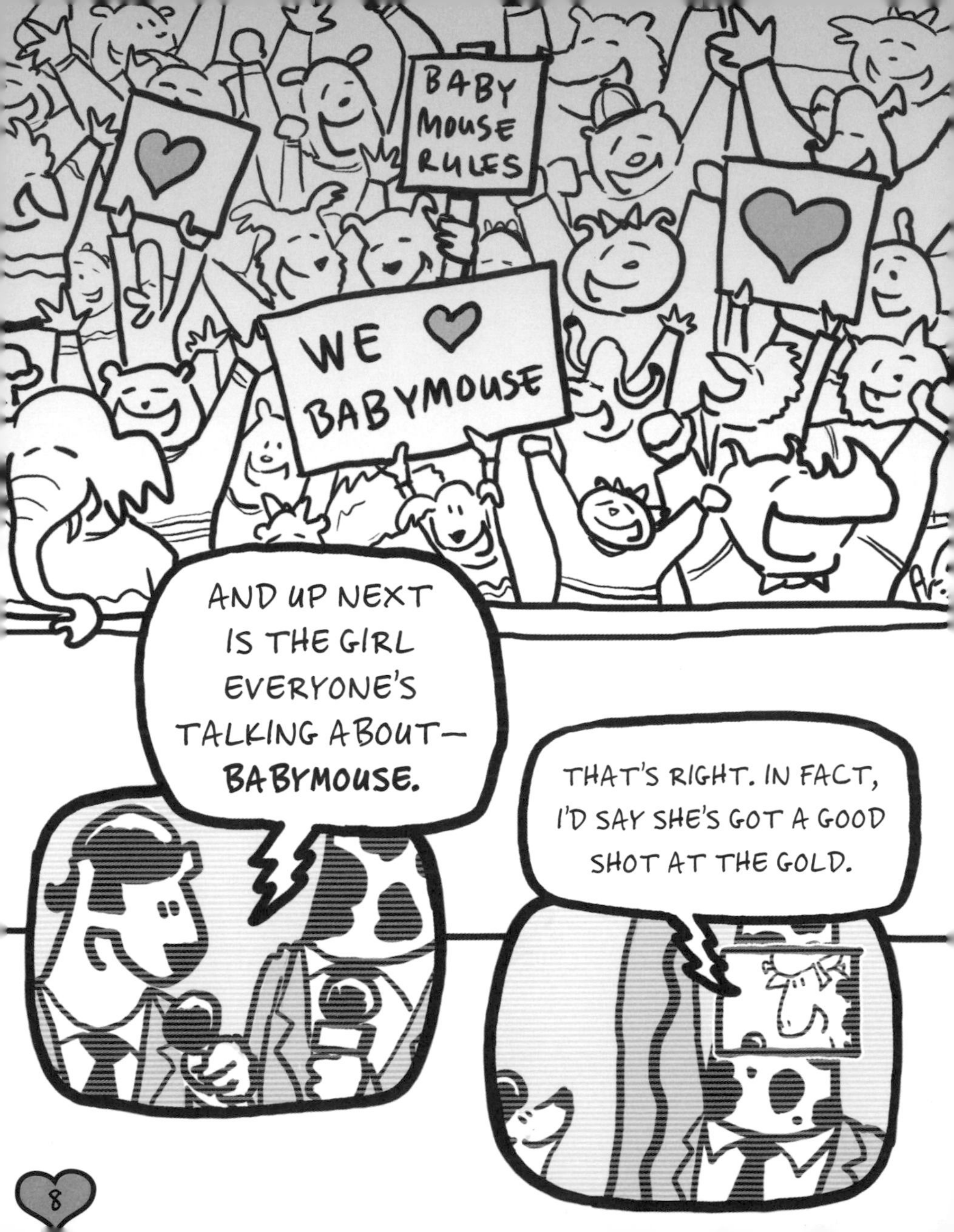
BABY MOUSE RULES
WE ♥ BABYMOUSE
AND UP NEXT IS THE GIRL EVERYONE'S TALKING ABOUT— BABYMOUSE.
THAT'S RIGHT. IN FACT, I'D SAY SHE'S GOT A GOOD SHOT AT THE GOLD.

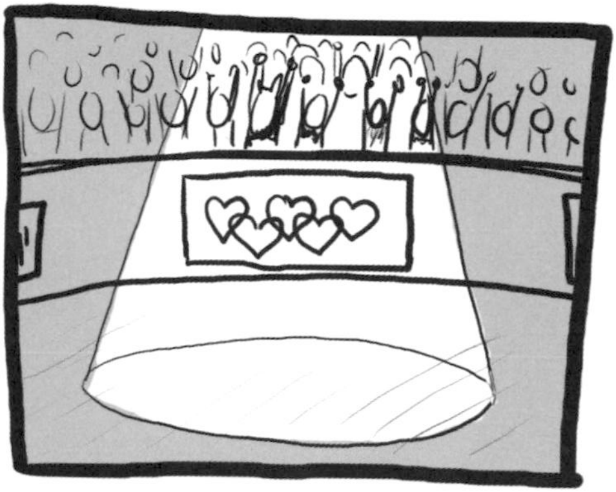

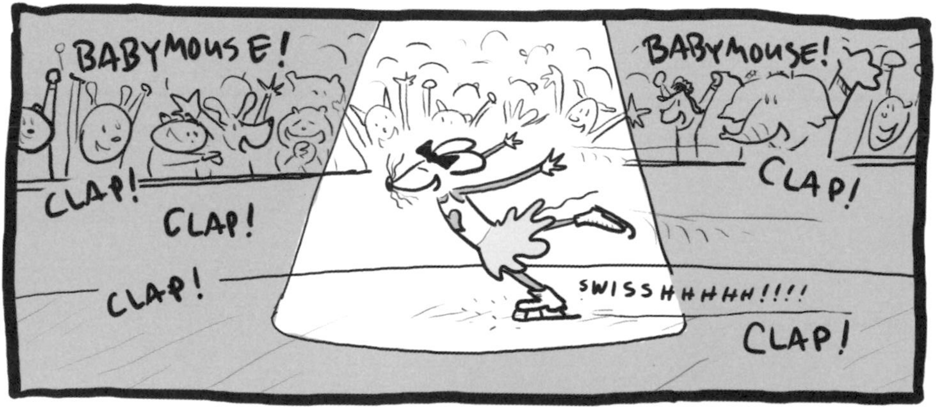
BABYMOUSE!
BABYMOUSE!
CLAP!
CLAP!
CLAP!
CLAP!
SWISSHHHHH!!!!
CLAP!

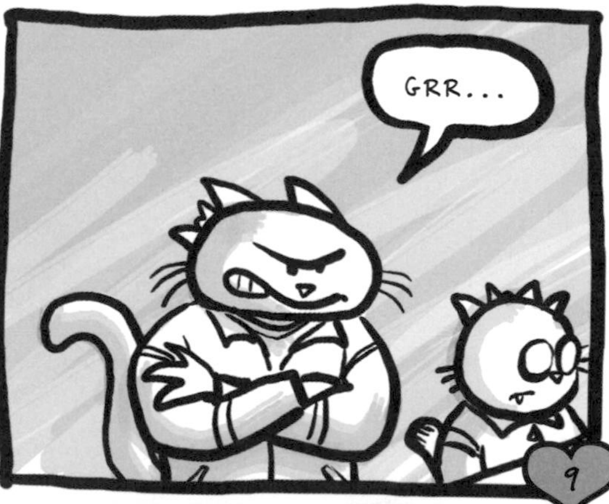
GRR...

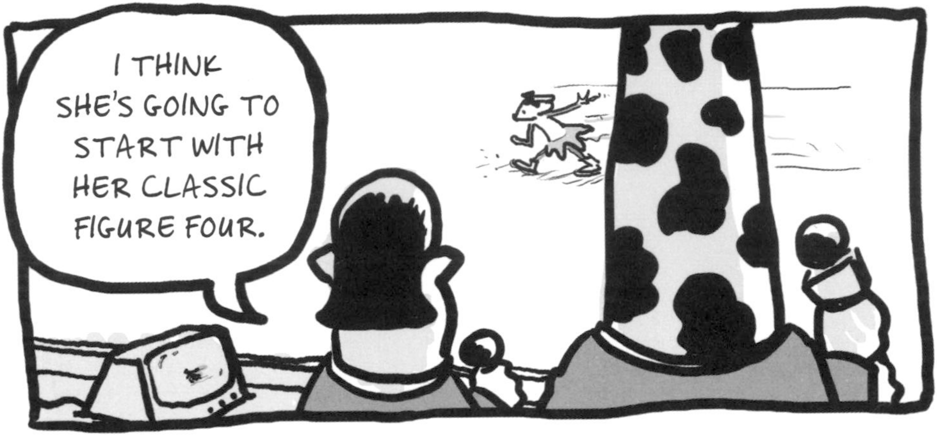
I THINK SHE'S GOING TO START WITH HER CLASSIC FIGURE FOUR.

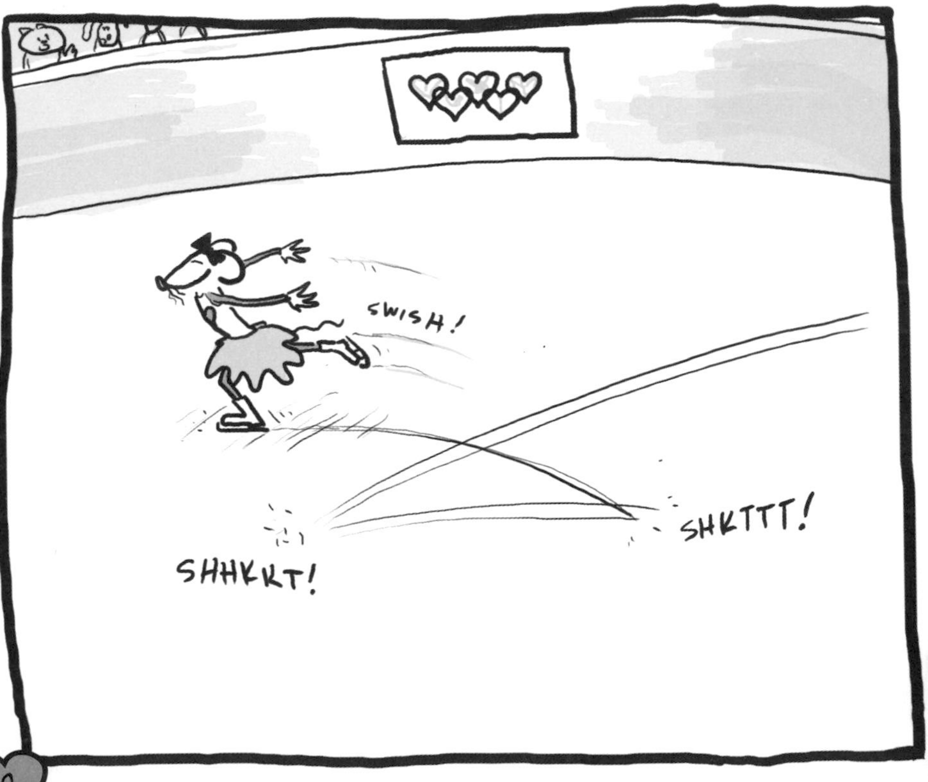
SWISH!
SHKTTT!
SHHKKT!

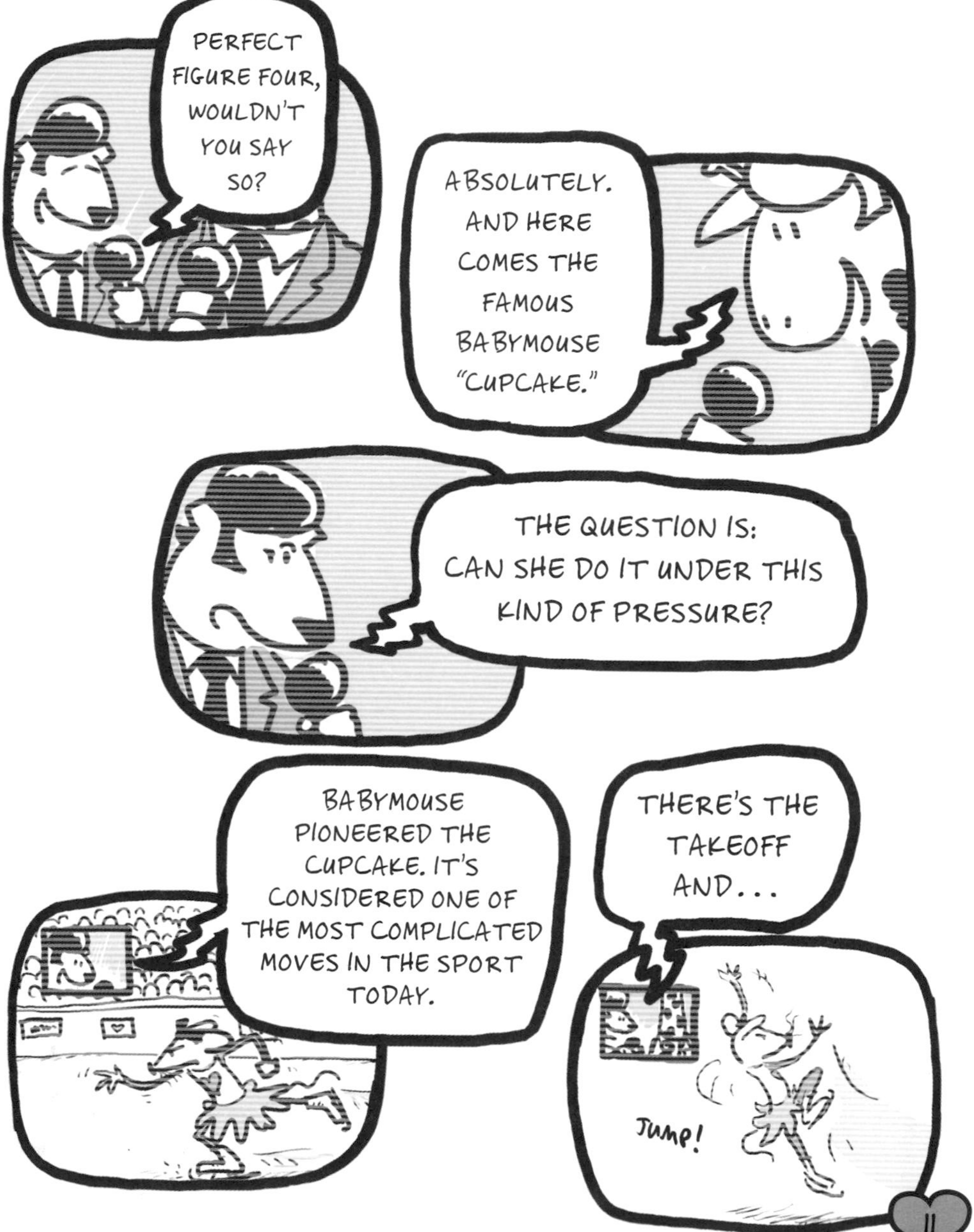
PERFECT FIGURE FOUR, WOULDN'T YOU SAY SO?
ABSOLUTELY. AND HERE COMES THE FAMOUS BABYMOUSE "CUPCAKE."
THE QUESTION IS: CAN SHE DO IT UNDER THIS KIND OF PRESSURE?
BABYMOUSE PIONEERED THE CUPCAKE. IT'S CONSIDERED ONE OF THE MOST COMPLICATED MOVES IN THE SPORT TODAY.
THERE'S THE TAKEOFF AND . . .
JUMP!

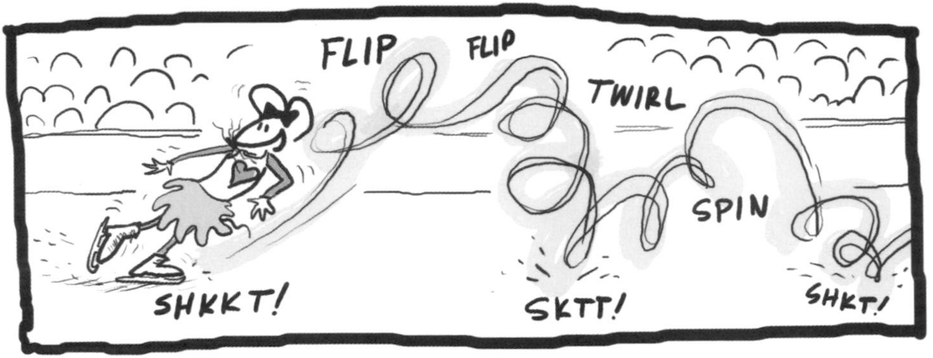
FLIP
FLIP
TWIRL
SPIN
SHKKT!
SKTT!
SHKT!

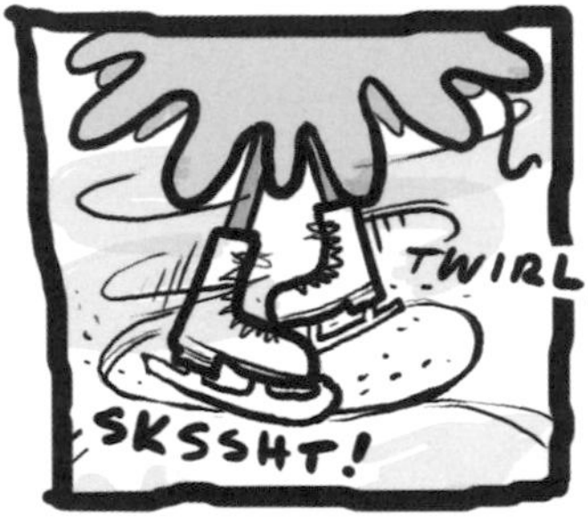
TWIRL!
SKSSHT!

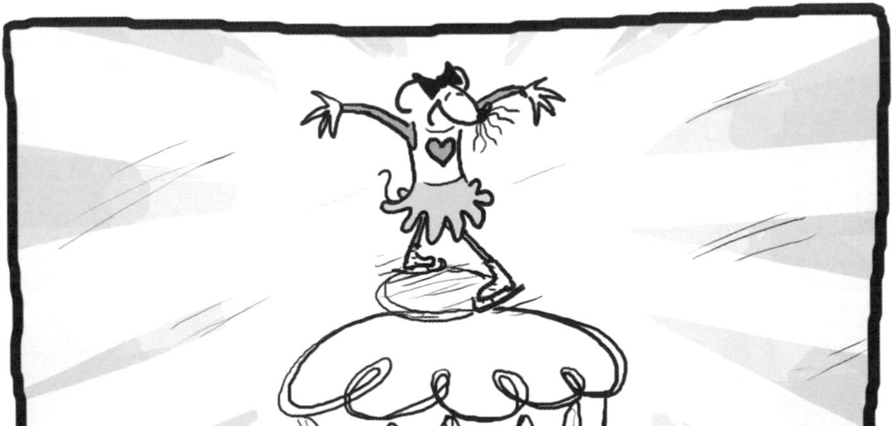

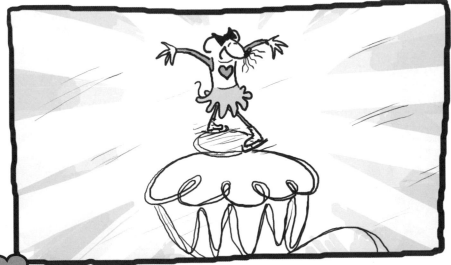

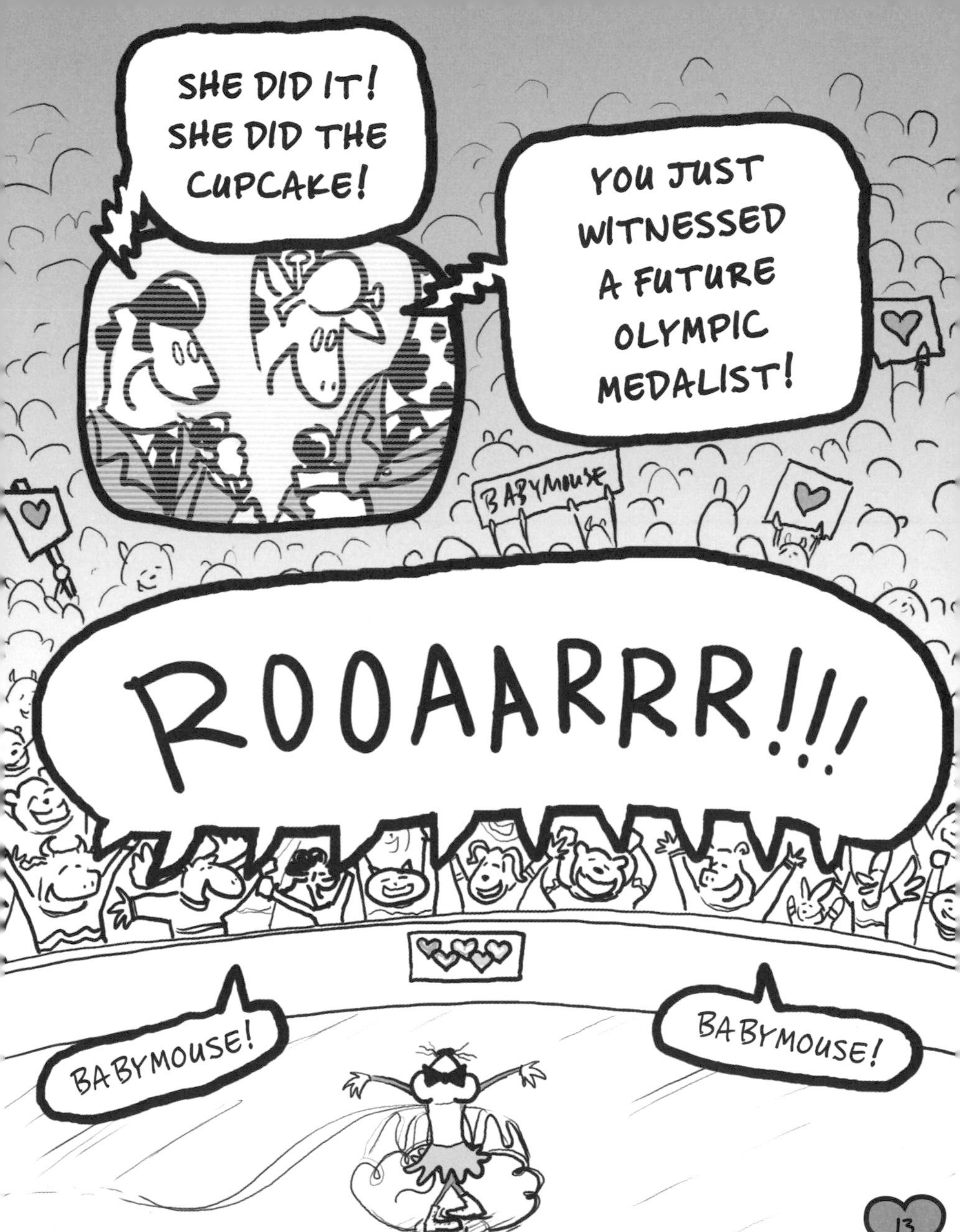
SHE DID IT! SHE DID THE CUPCAKE!
YOU JUST WITNESSED A FUTURE OLYMPIC MEDALIST!
BABYMOUSE
ROOAARRR!!!
BABYMOUSE!
BABYMOUSE!

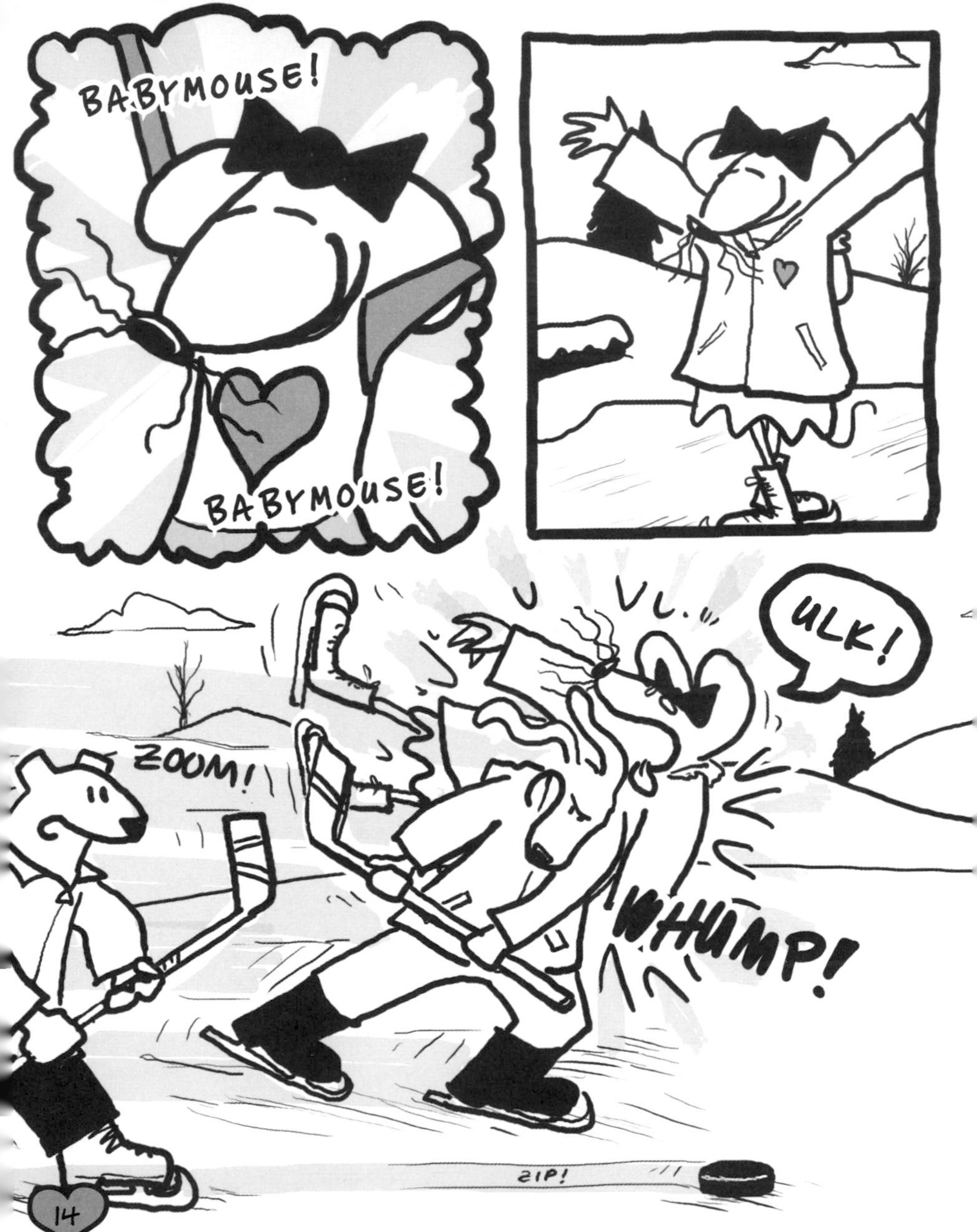
BABYMOUSE!
BABYMOUSE!
ZOOM!
ULK!
WHUMP!
ZIP!

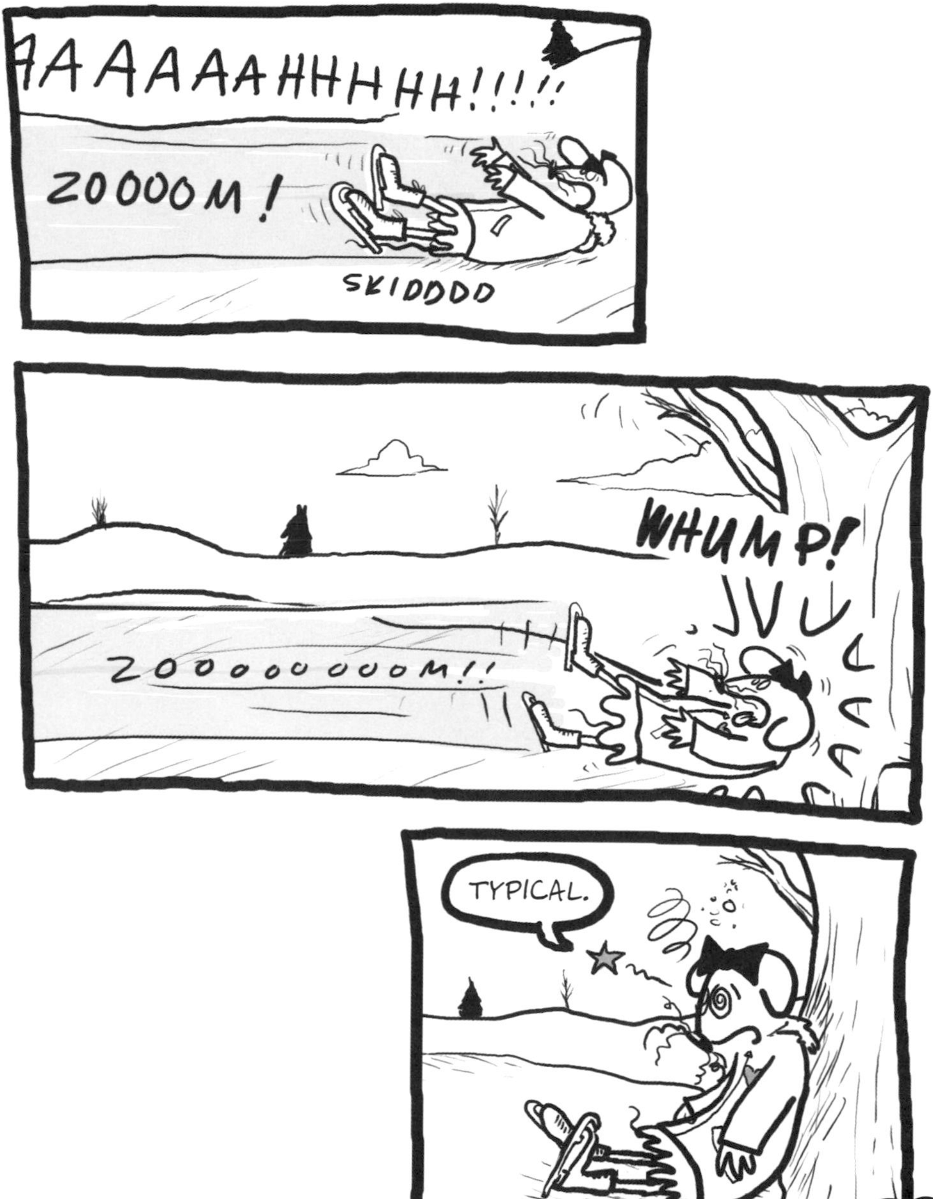
AAAAAAHHHHH!!!!!
ZOOOOM!
SKIDDDD
WHUMP!
ZOOOOOOOOOOM!!
TYPICAL.

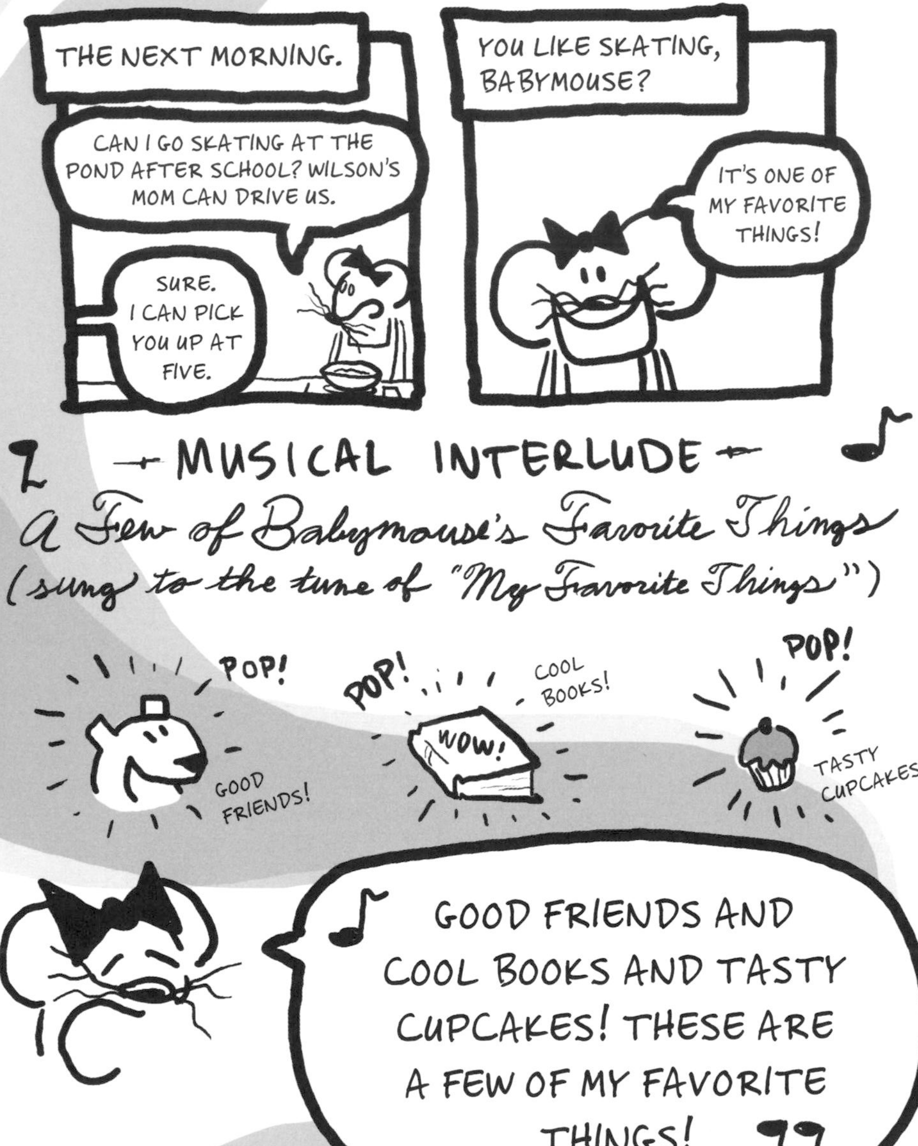
THE NEXT MORNING.
CAN I GO SKATING AT THE POND AFTER SCHOOL? WILSON'S MOM CAN DRIVE US.
SURE. I CAN PICK YOU UP AT FIVE.
YOU LIKE SKATING, BABYMOUSE?
IT'S ONE OF MY FAVORITE THINGS!
MUSICAL INTERLUDE
A Few of Babymouse's Favorite Things
(sung to the tune of "My Favorite Things")
POP!
GOOD FRIENDS!
POP!
WOW!
COOL BOOKS!
POP!
TASTY CUPCAKES!
GOOD FRIENDS AND COOL BOOKS AND TASTY CUPCAKES! THESE ARE A FEW OF MY FAVORITE THINGS!

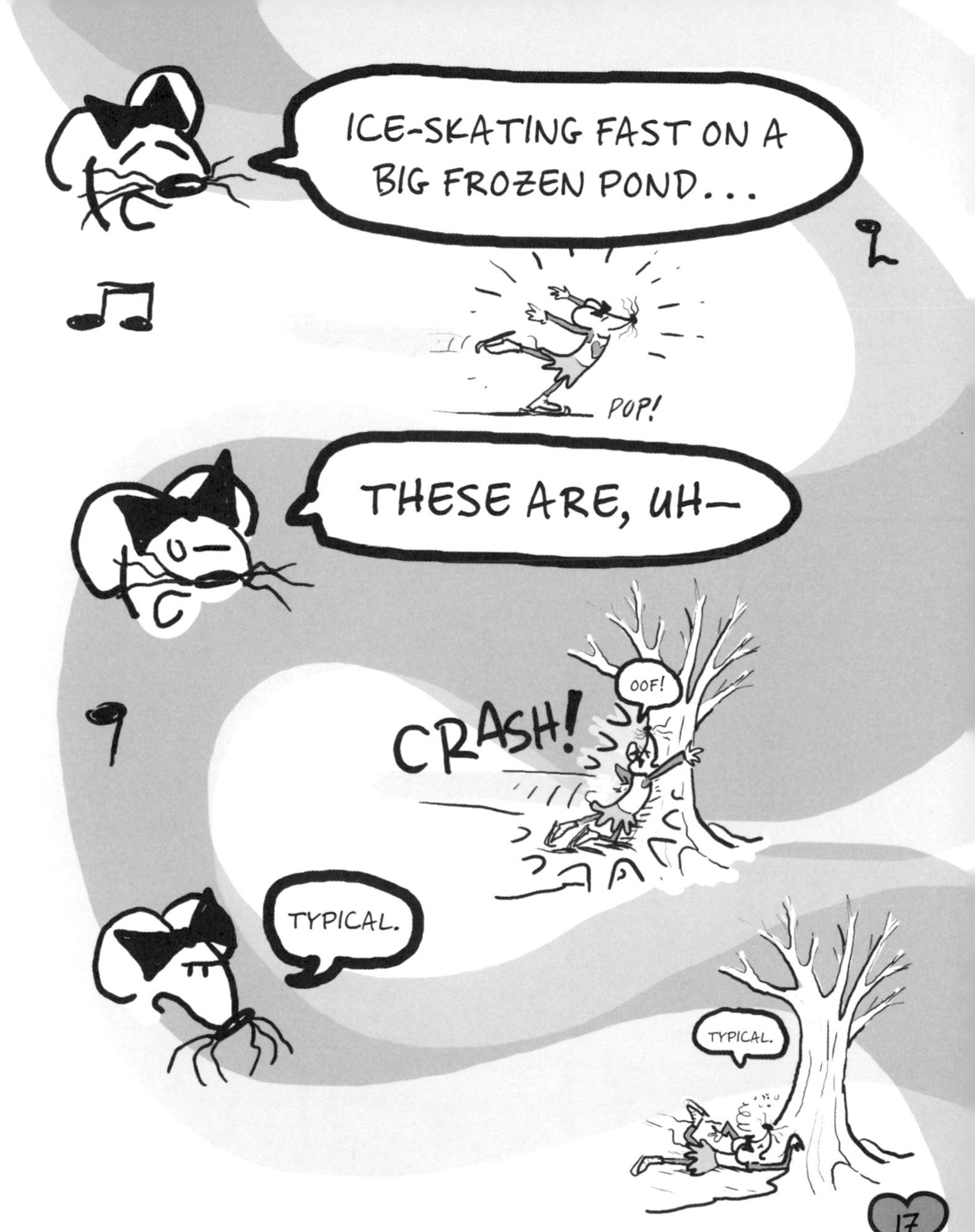
ICE-SKATING FAST ON A BIG FROZEN POND...
POP!
THESE ARE, UH—
OOF!
CRASH!
TYPICAL.
TYPICAL.

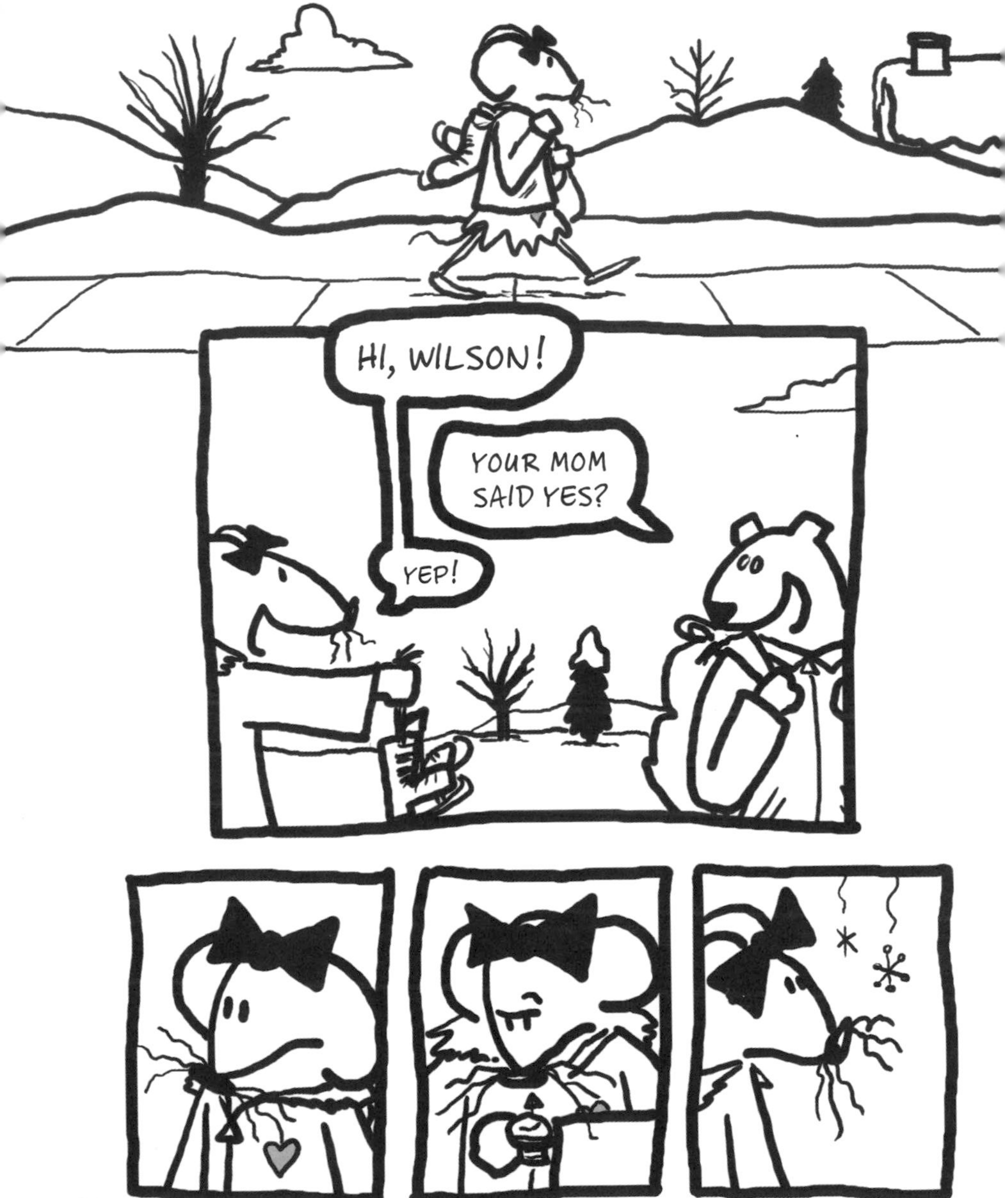
HI, WILSON!
YOUR MOM SAID YES?
YEP!

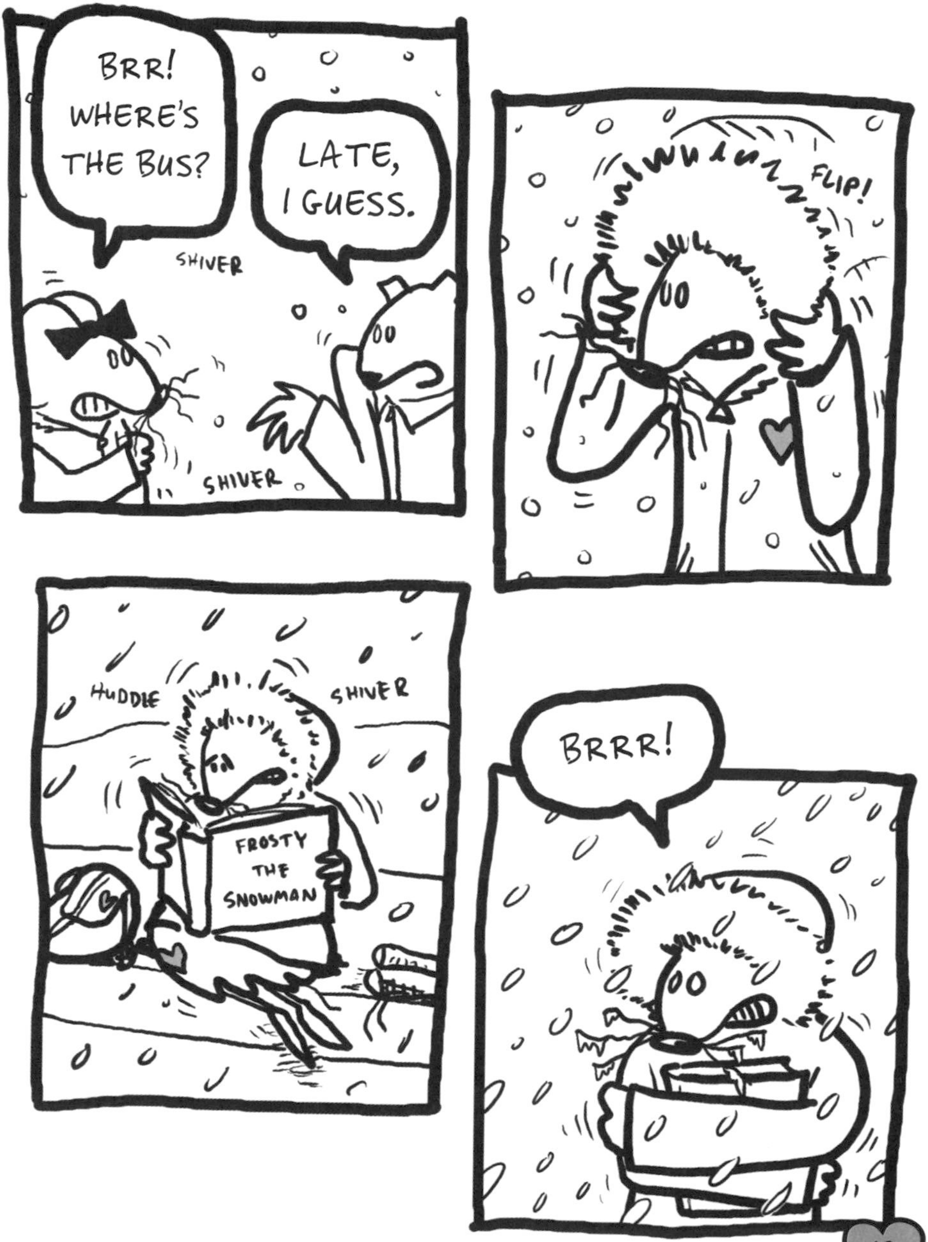
BRR! WHERE'S THE BUS?
LATE, I GUESS.
SHIVER
SHIVER
FLIP!
HUDDLE
SHIVER
FROSTY THE SNOWMAN
BRRR!

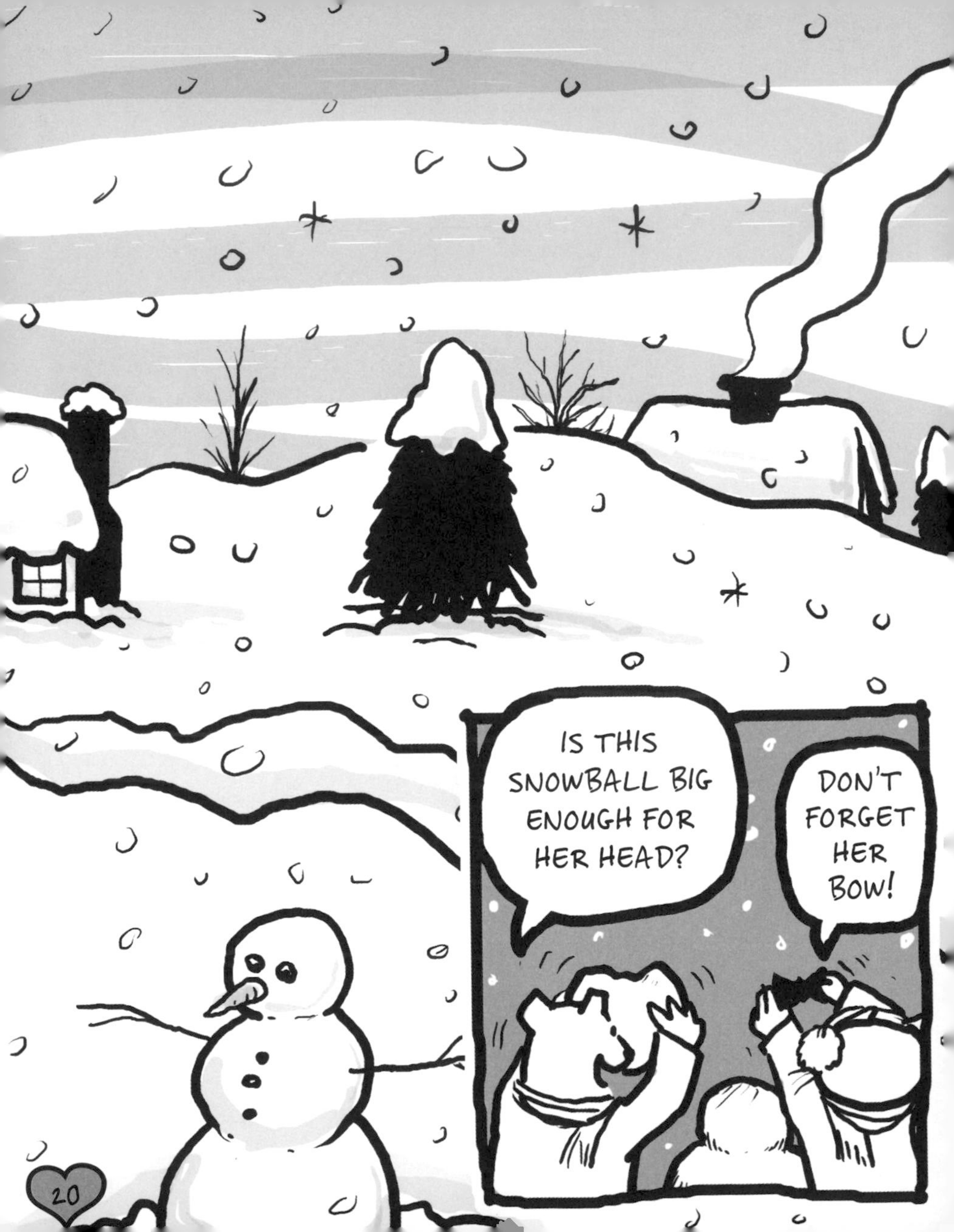
IS THIS SNOWBALL BIG ENOUGH FOR HER HEAD?
DON'T FORGET HER BOW!

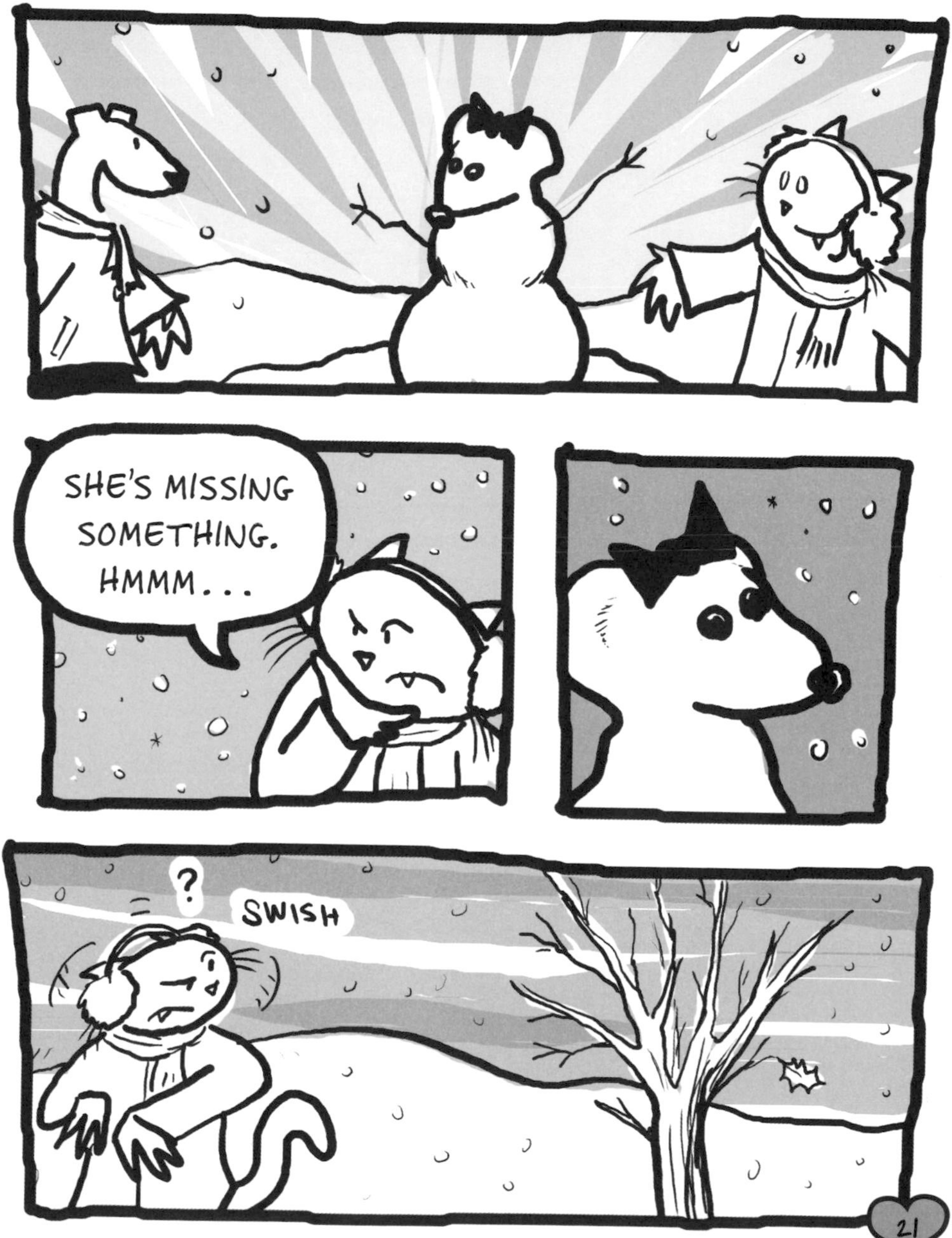
SHE'S MISSING SOMETHING. HMMM...
?
SWISH

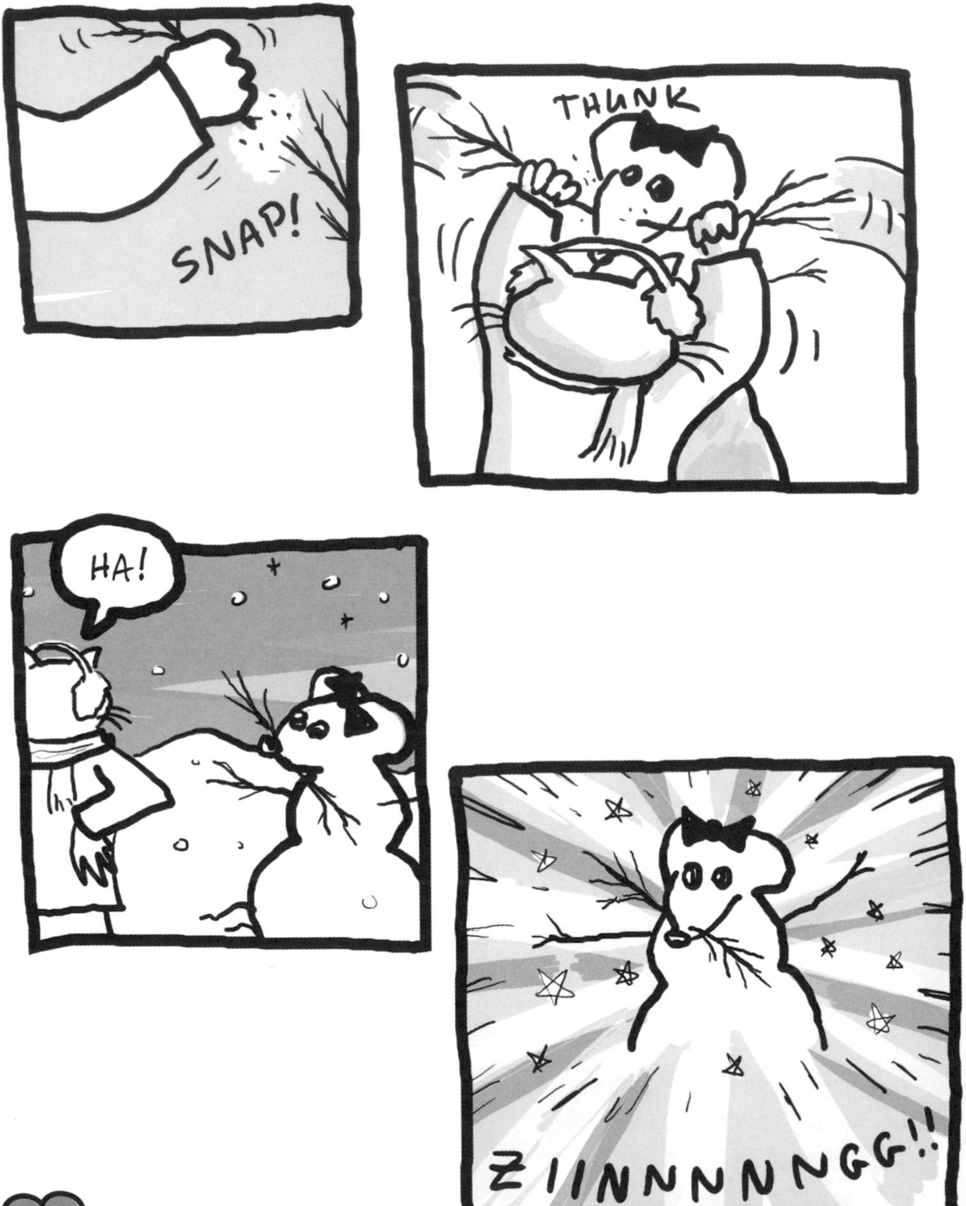
SNAP!
THUNK
HA!
ZIINNNNNGG!!

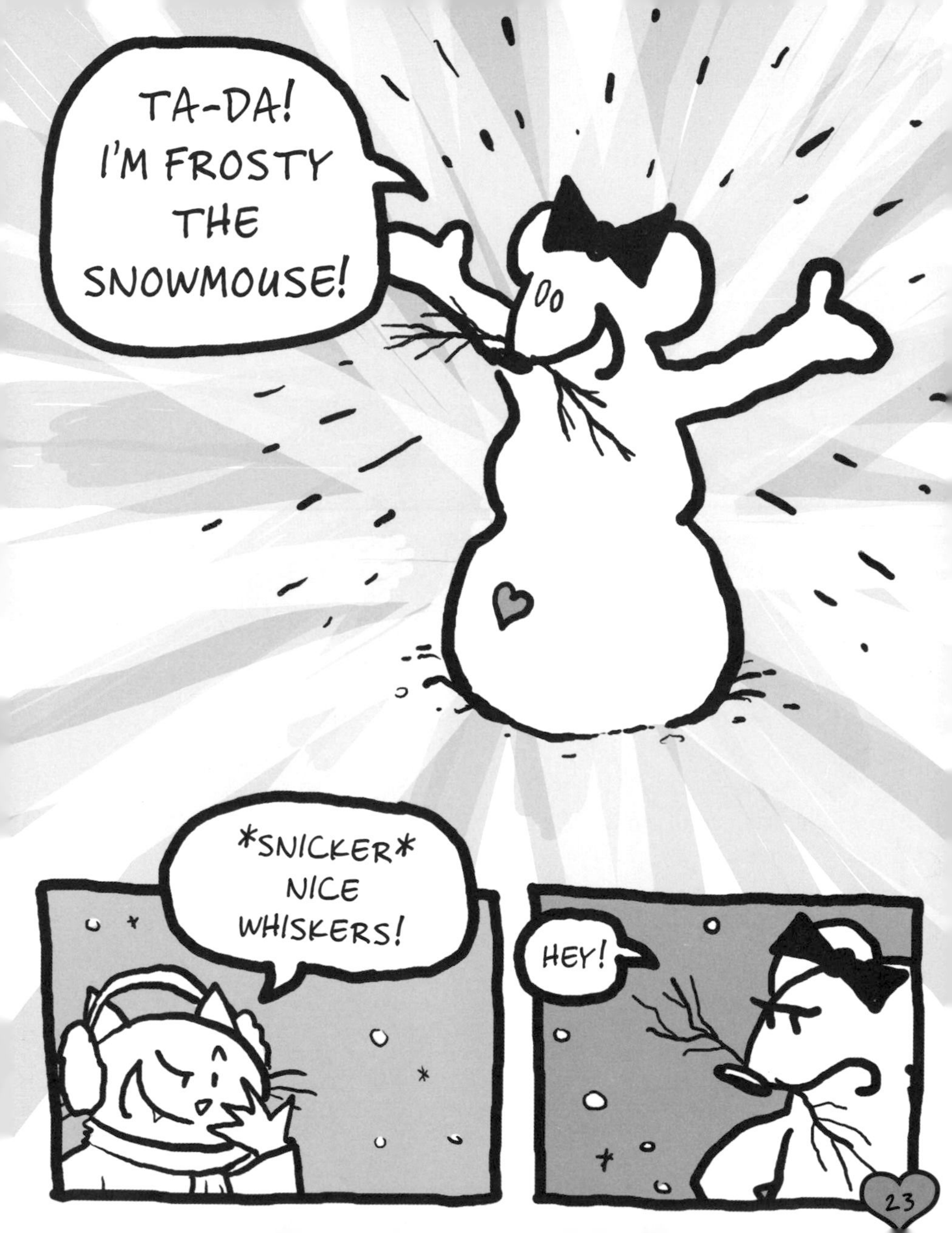
TA-DA! I'M FROSTY THE SNOWMOUSE!
SNICKER NICE WHISKERS!
HEY!

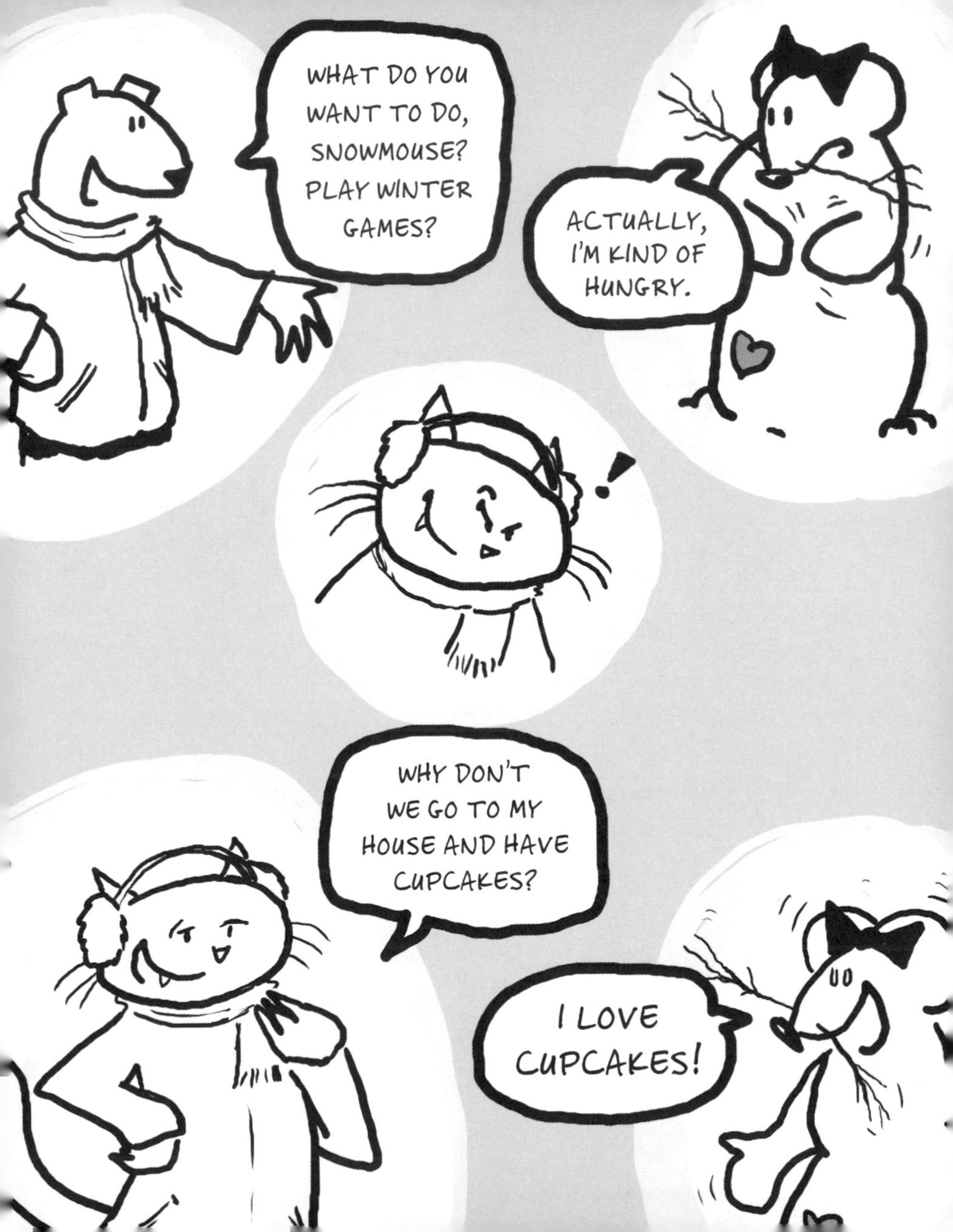
WHAT DO YOU WANT TO DO, SNOWMOUSE? PLAY WINTER GAMES?
ACTUALLY, I'M KIND OF HUNGRY.
WHY DON'T WE GO TO MY HOUSE AND HAVE CUPCAKES?
I LOVE CUPCAKES!

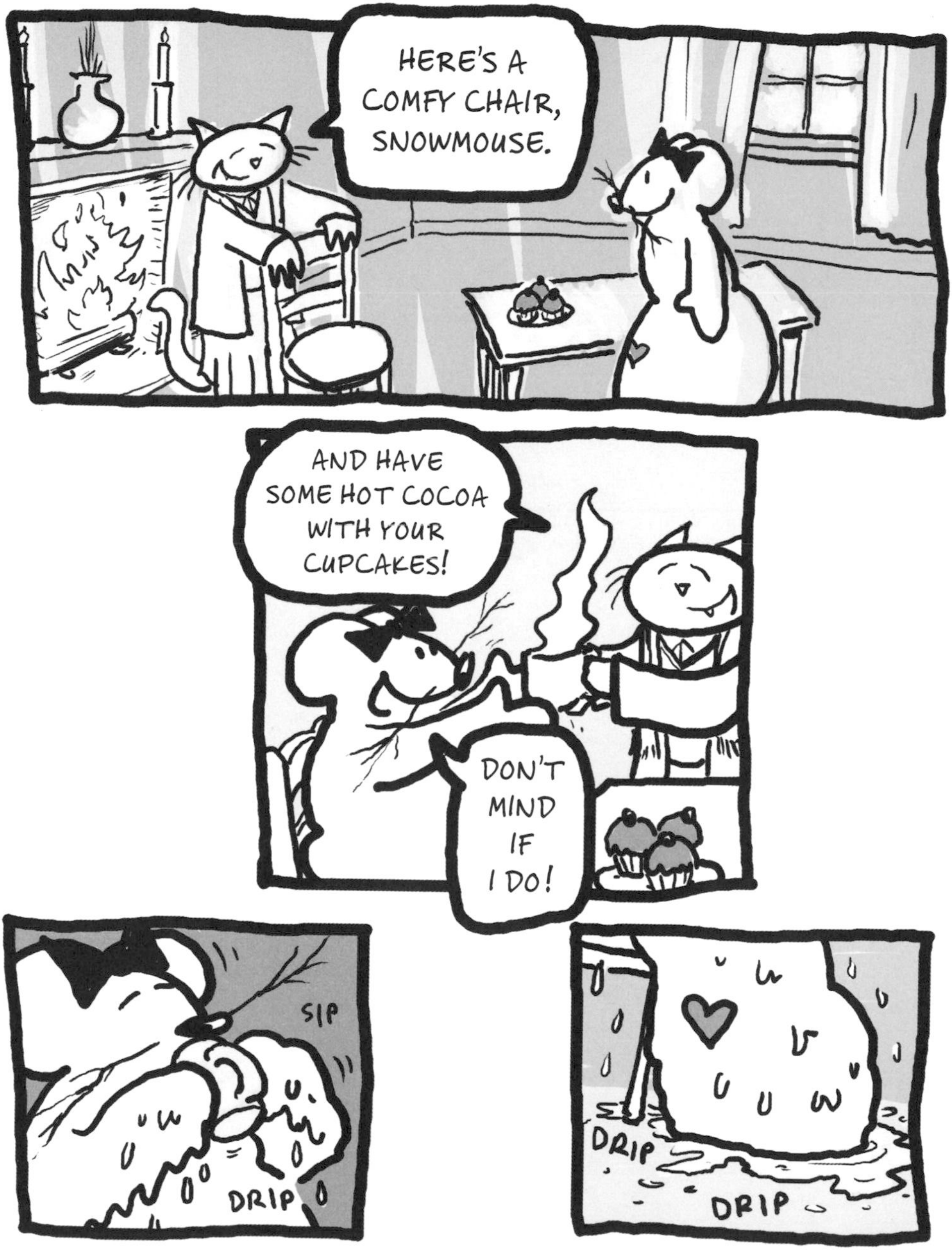
HERE'S A COMFY CHAIR, SNOWMOUSE.
AND HAVE SOME HOT COCOA WITH YOUR CUPCAKES!
DON'T MIND IF I DO!
SIP
DRIP
DRIP
DRIP

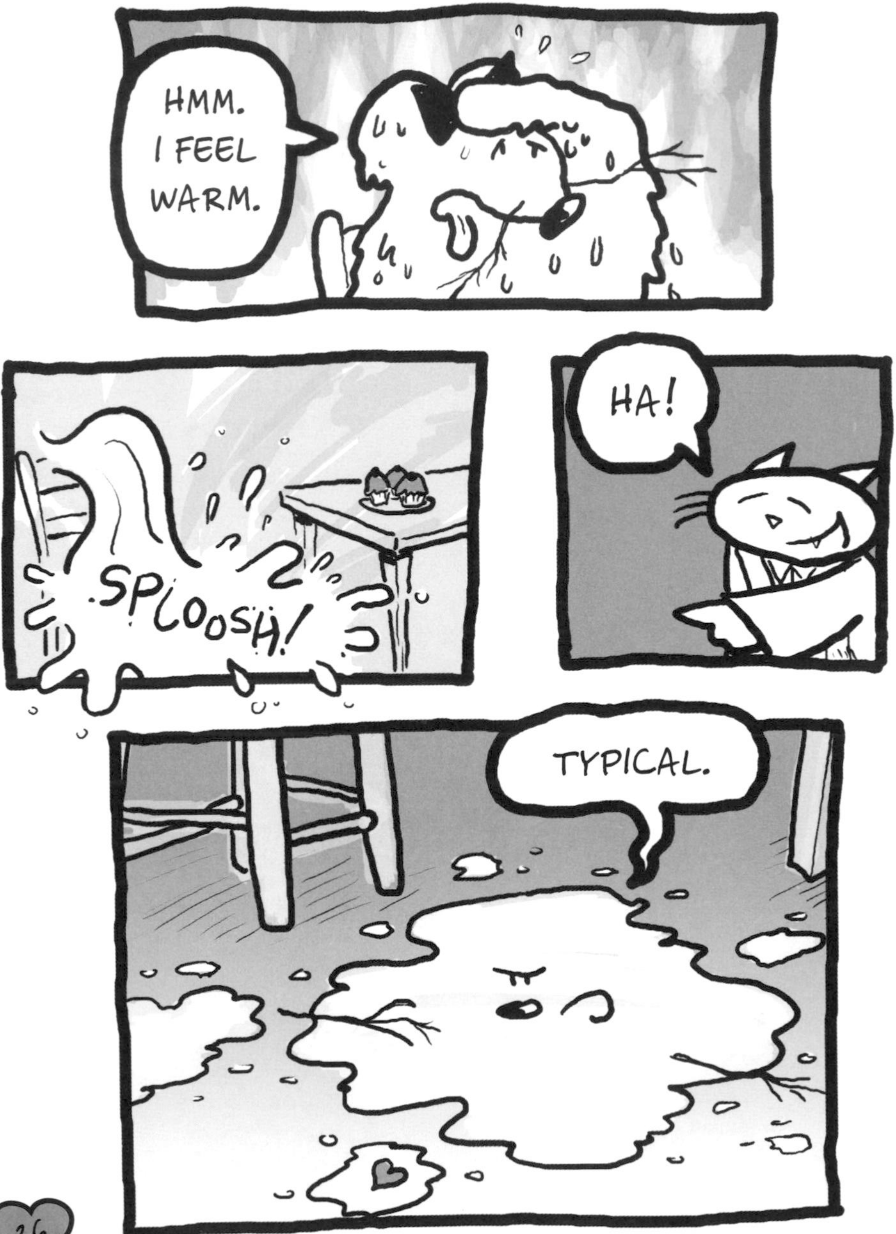
HMM. I FEEL WARM.
SPLOOSH!
HA!
TYPICAL.

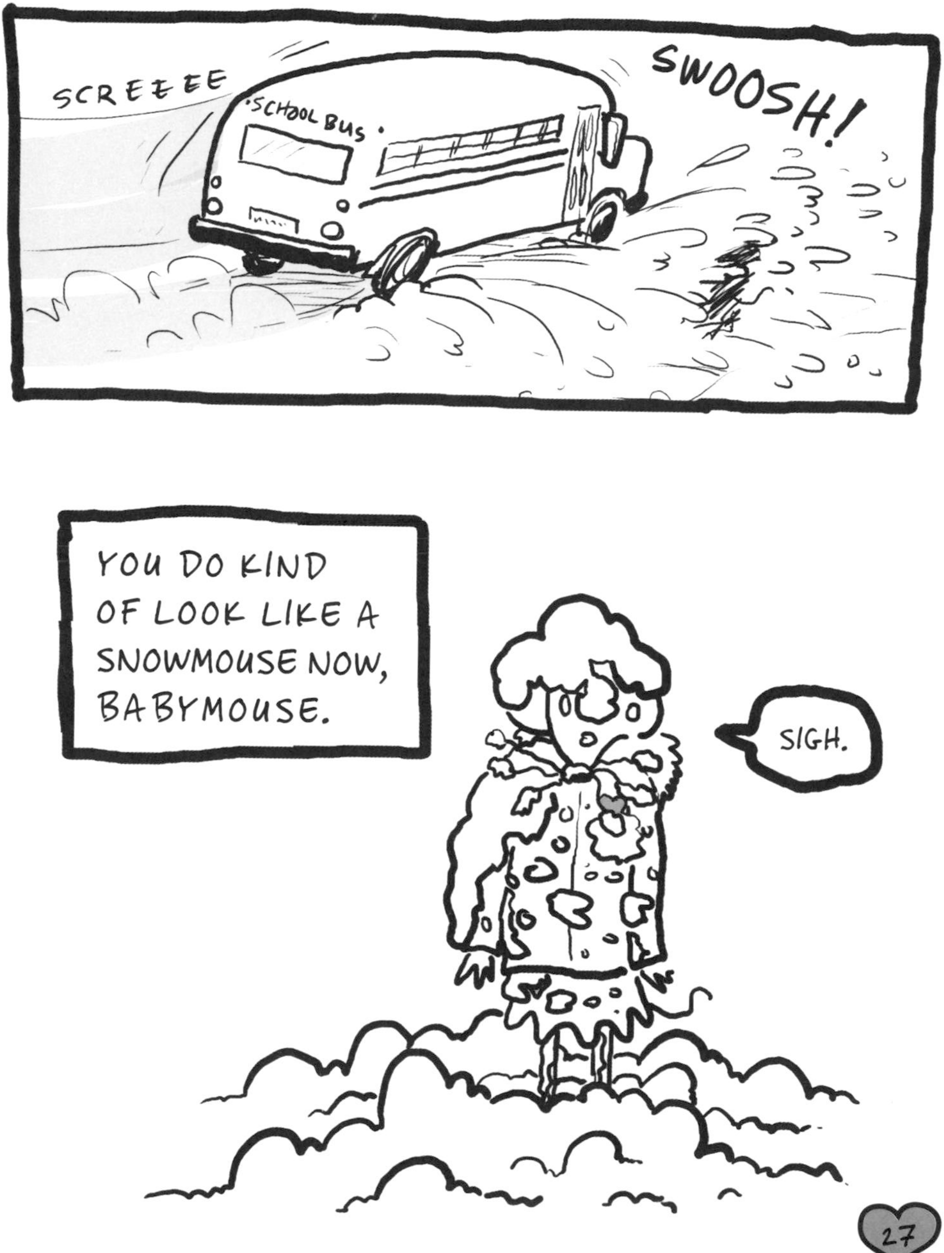
SCREEEEE
SCHOOL BUS
SWOOSH!
YOU DO KIND OF LOOK LIKE A SNOWMOUSE NOW, BABYMOUSE.
SIGH.

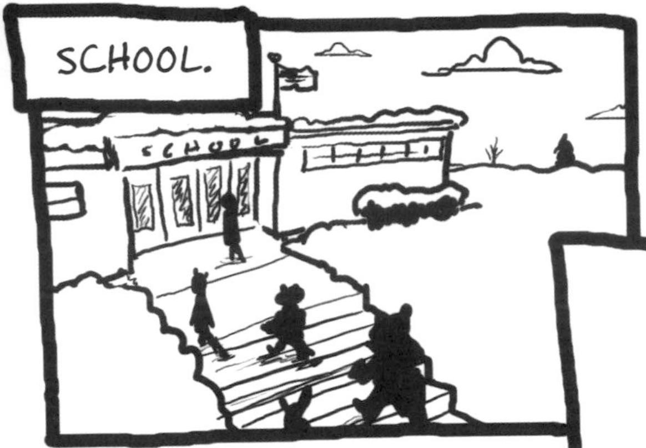
SCHOOL.
SCHOOL

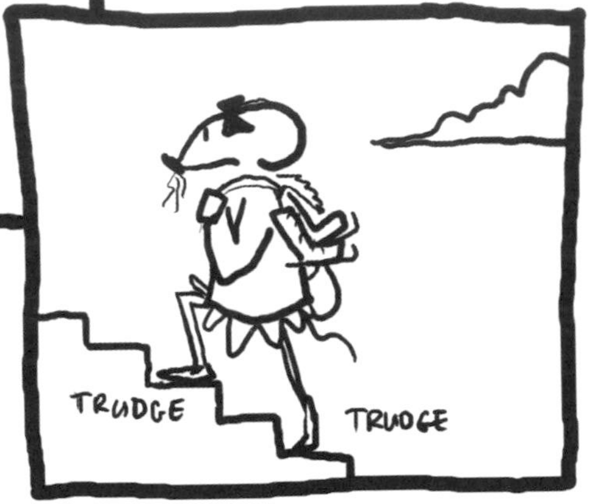
TRUDGE
TRUDGE

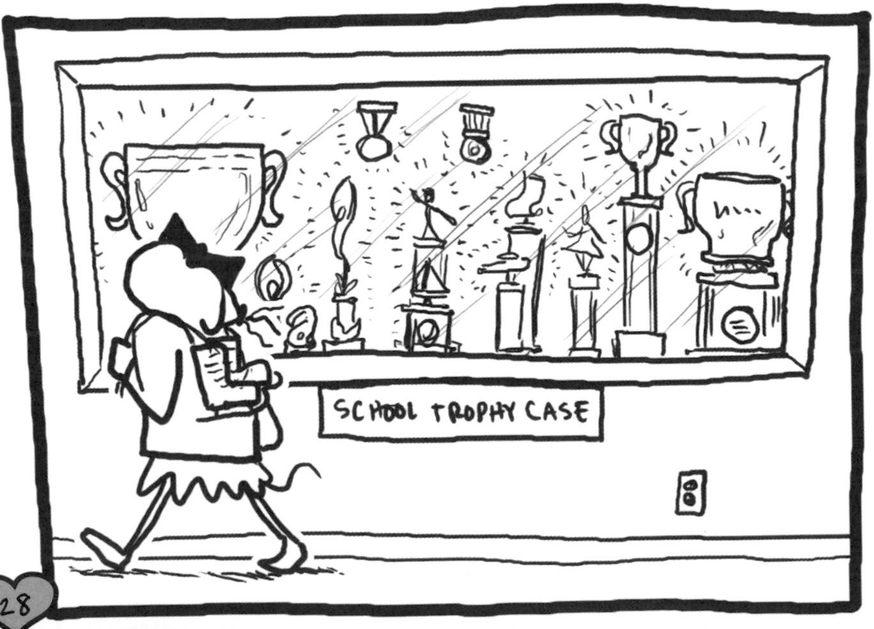
SCHOOL TROPHY CASE

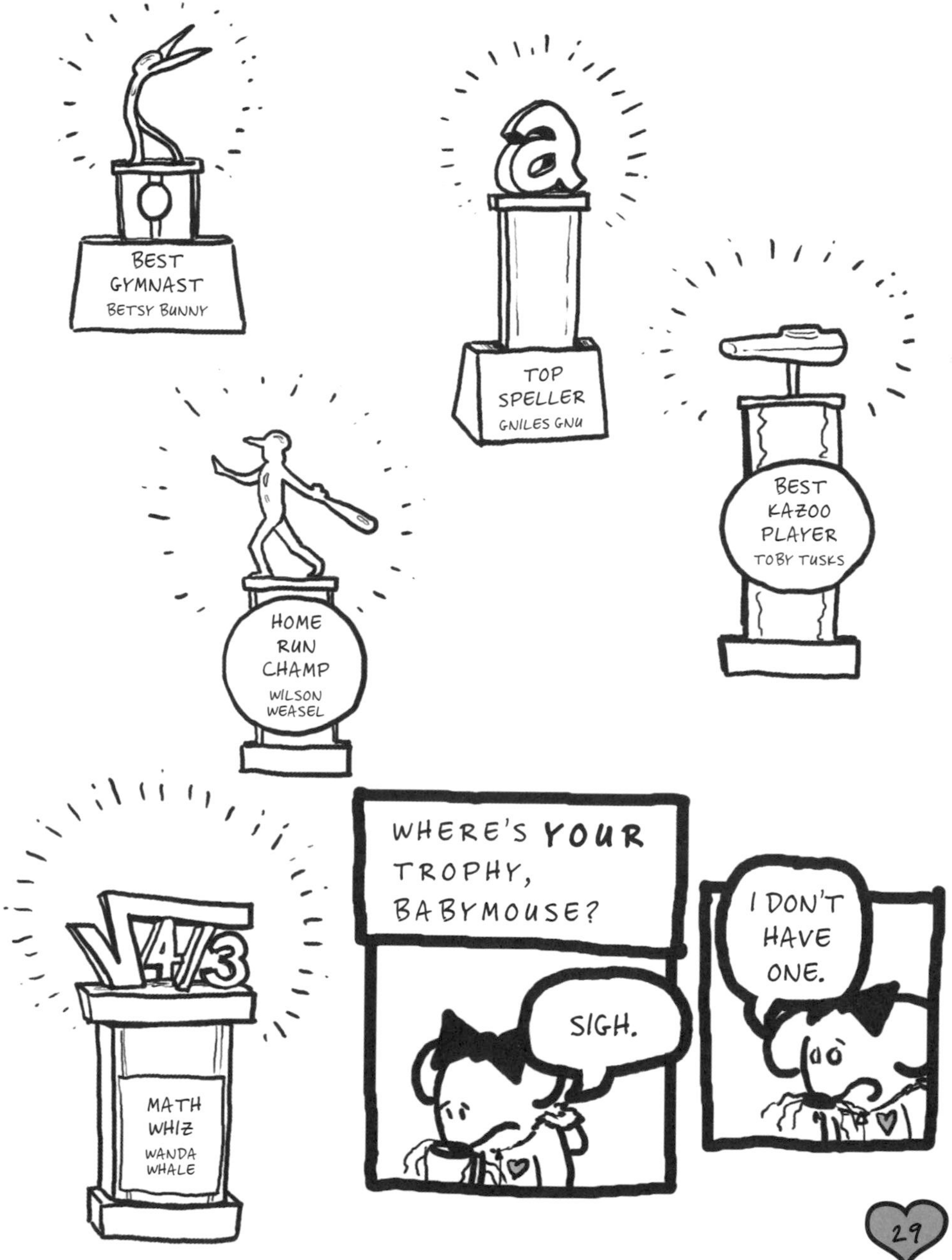
BEST GYMNAST
BETSY BUNNY
TOP SPELLER
GNILES GNU
BEST KAZOO PLAYER
TOBY TUSKS
HOME RUN CHAMP
WILSON WEASEL
MATH WHIZ
WANDA WHALE
WHERE'S **YOUR** TROPHY, BABYMOUSE?
SIGH.
I DON'T HAVE ONE.

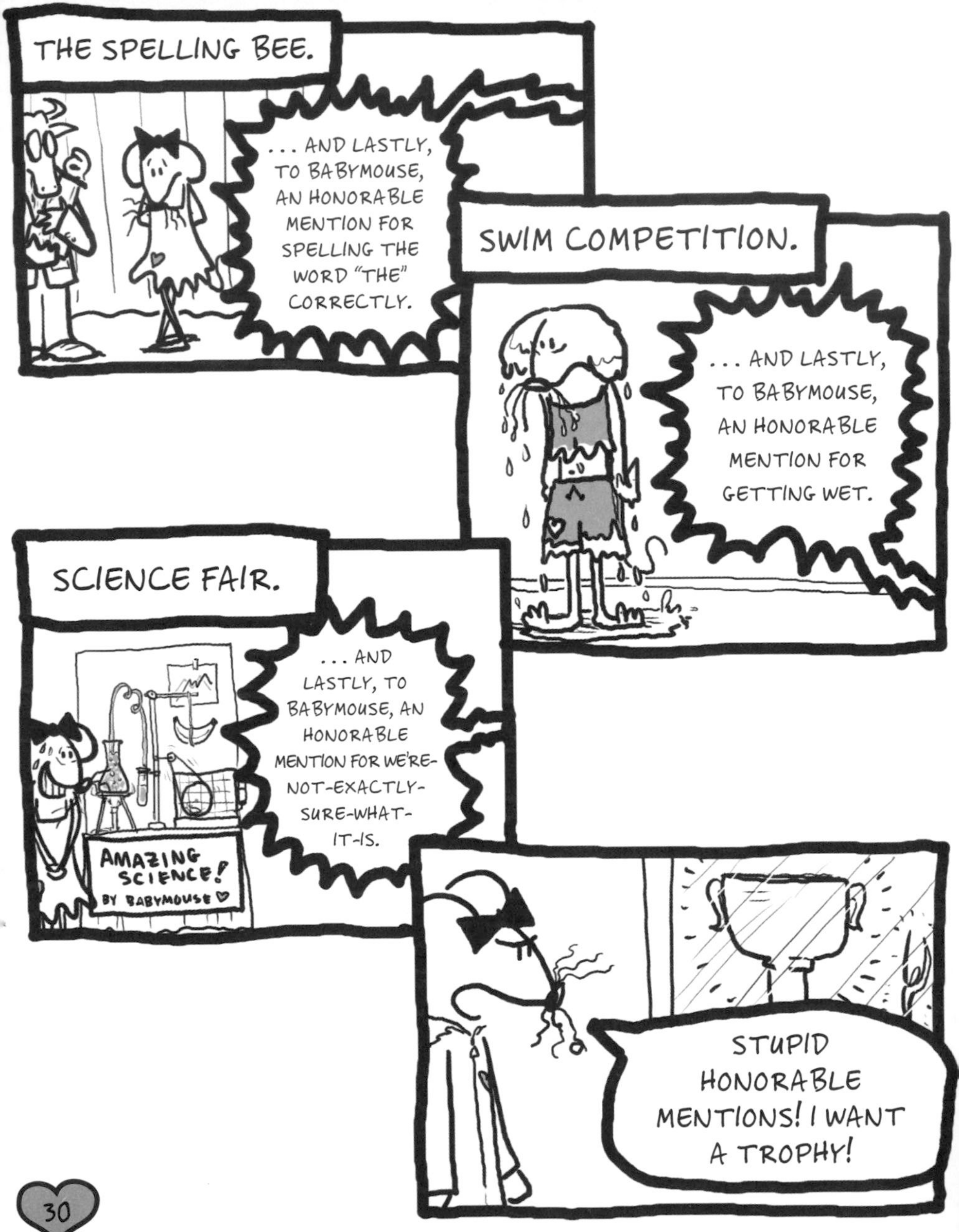
THE SPELLING BEE.
. . . AND LASTLY, TO BABYMOUSE, AN HONORABLE MENTION FOR SPELLING THE WORD "THE" CORRECTLY.
SWIM COMPETITION.
. . . AND LASTLY, TO BABYMOUSE, AN HONORABLE MENTION FOR GETTING WET.
SCIENCE FAIR.
. . . AND LASTLY, TO BABYMOUSE, AN HONORABLE MENTION FOR WE'RE-NOT-EXACTLY-SURE-WHAT-IT-IS.
AMAZING SCIENCE!
BY BABYMOUSE ♡
STUPID HONORABLE MENTIONS! I WANT A TROPHY!

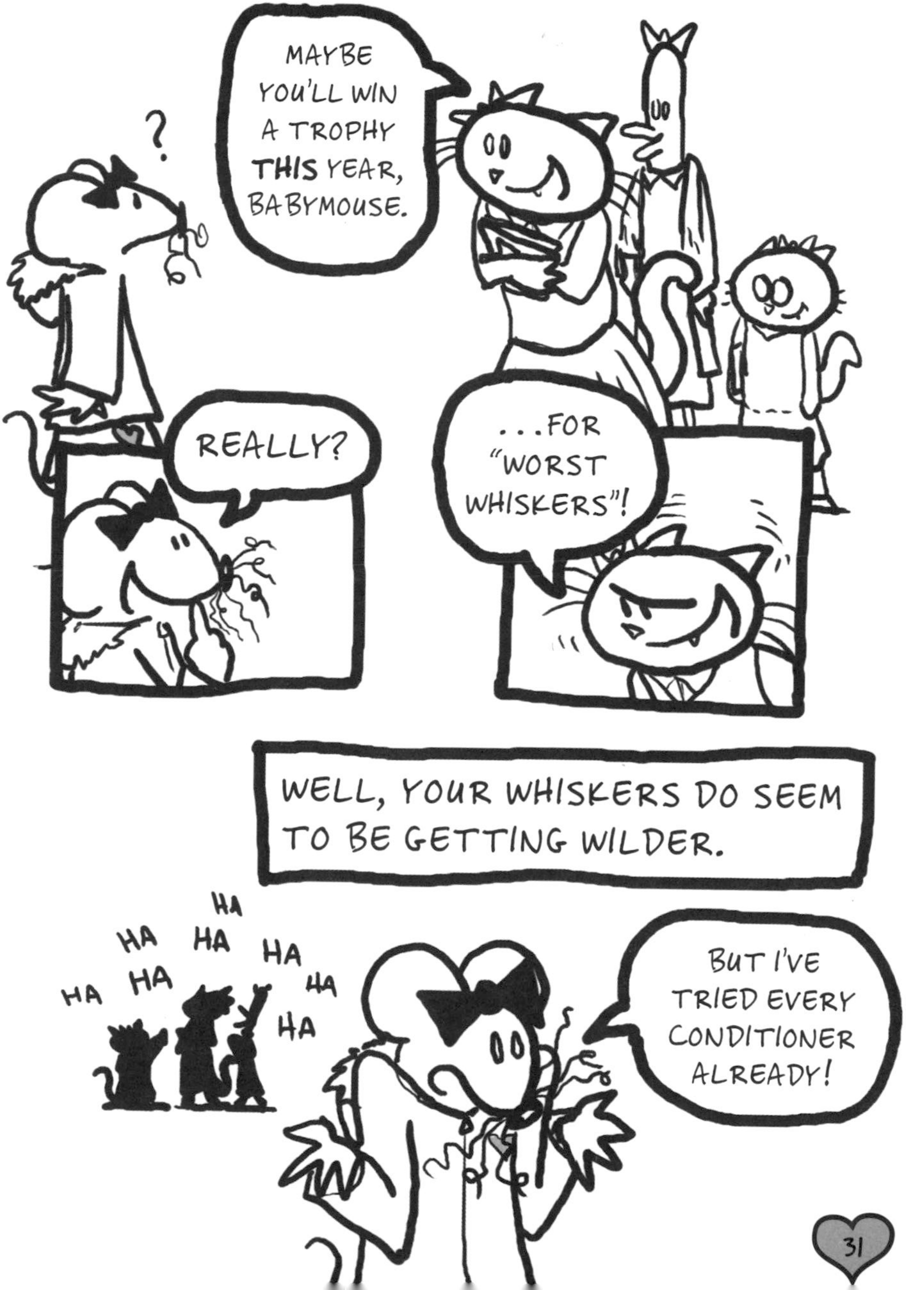
?
MAYBE YOU'LL WIN A TROPHY **THIS** YEAR, BABYMOUSE.
REALLY?
...FOR "WORST WHISKERS"!
WELL, YOUR WHISKERS DO SEEM TO BE GETTING WILDER.
HA HA HA HA HA HA HA HA
BUT I'VE TRIED EVERY CONDITIONER ALREADY!

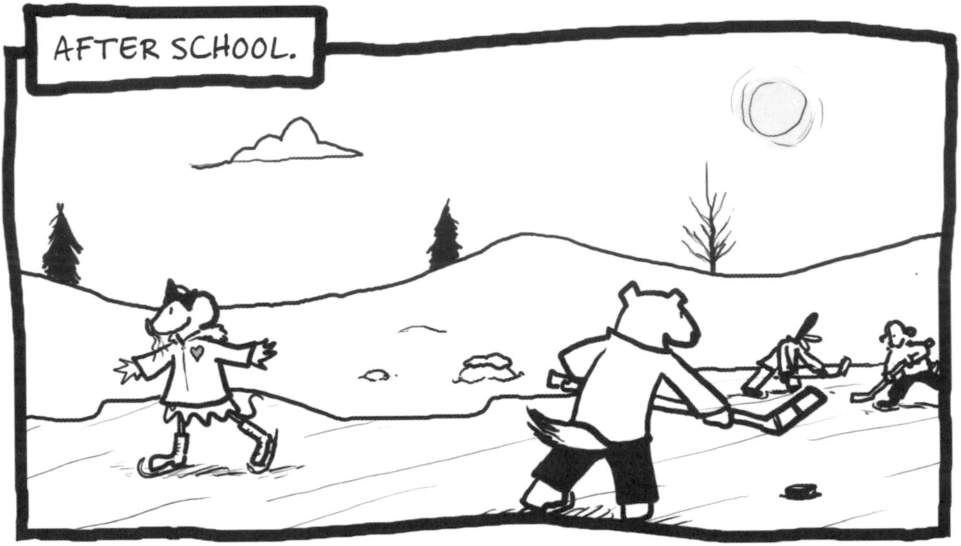
AFTER SCHOOL.

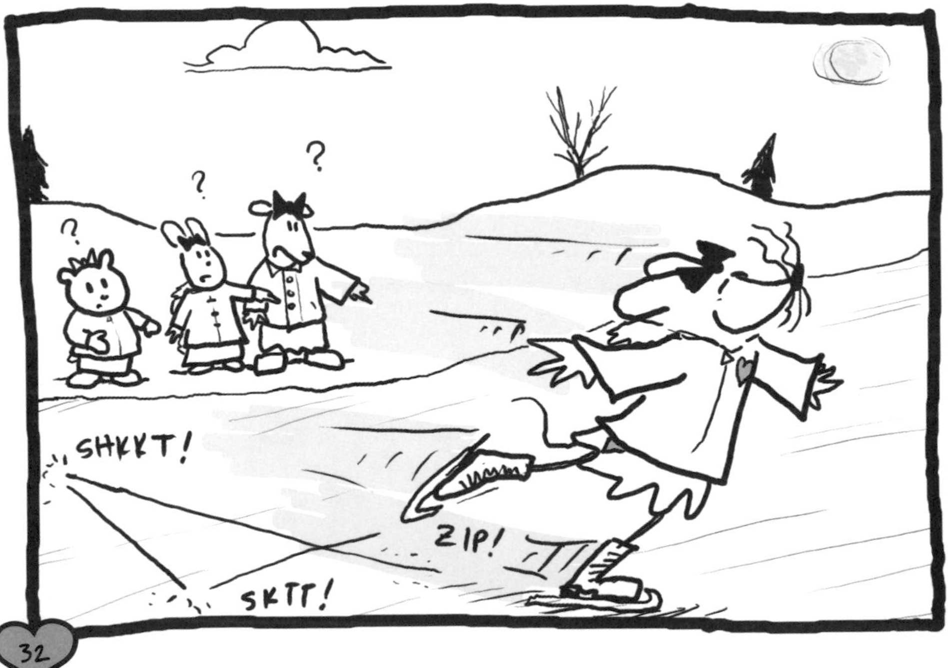
SHKKT!
ZIP!
SKTT!

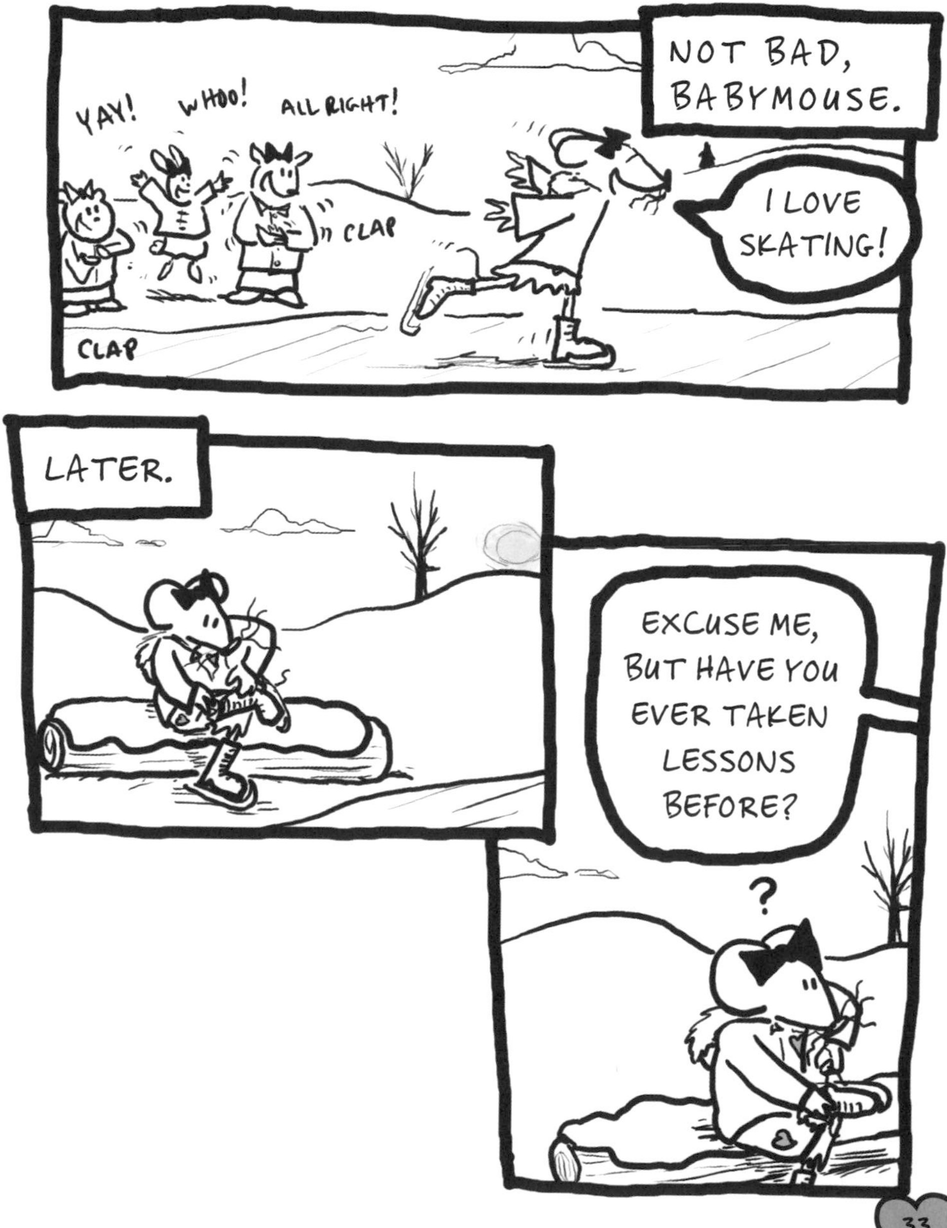
NOT BAD, BABYMOUSE.
YAY!
WHOO!
ALL RIGHT!
CLAP
CLAP
I LOVE SKATING!
LATER.
EXCUSE ME, BUT HAVE YOU EVER TAKEN LESSONS BEFORE?
?

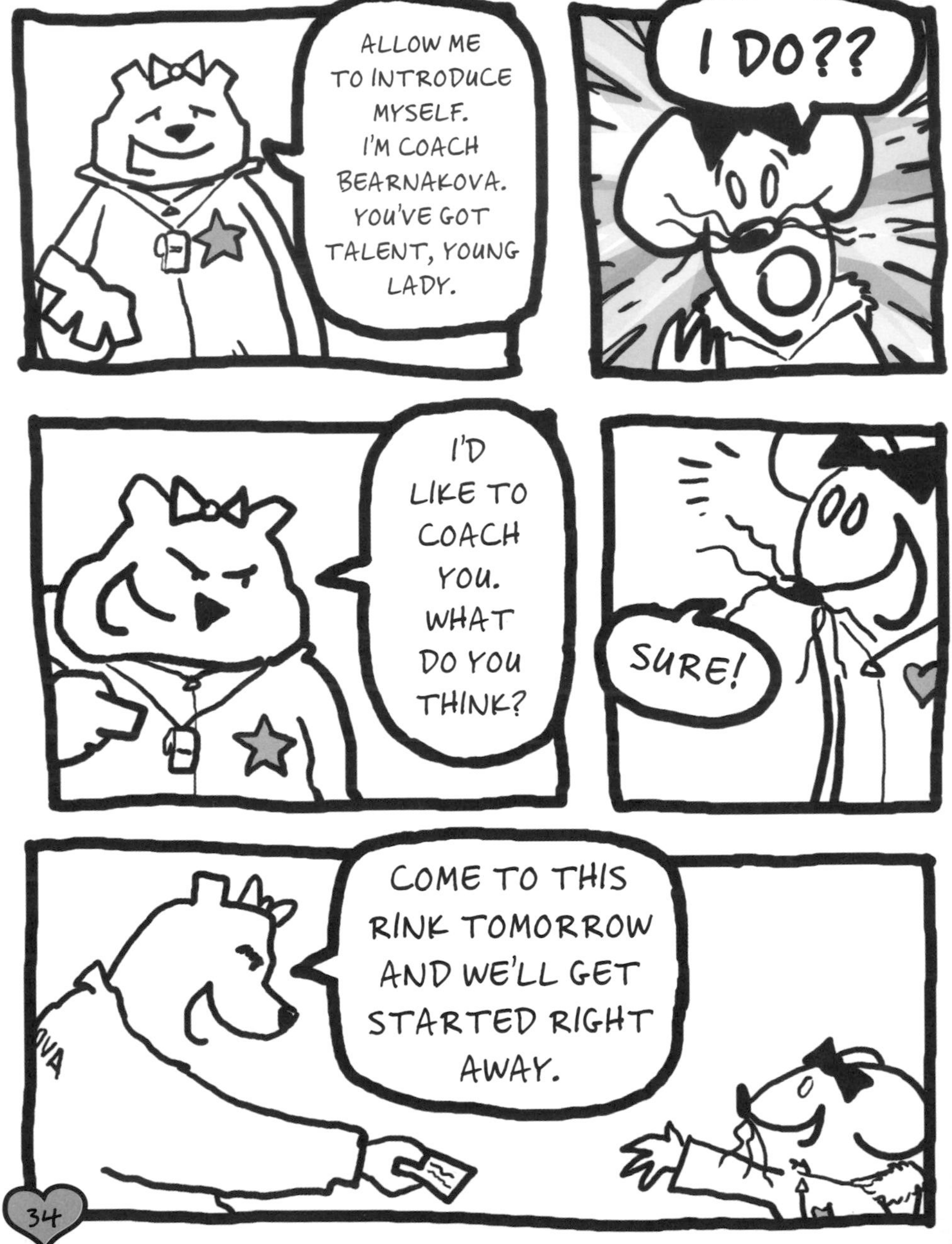
ALLOW ME TO INTRODUCE MYSELF. I'M COACH BEARNAKOVA. YOU'VE GOT TALENT, YOUNG LADY.
I DO??
I'D LIKE TO COACH YOU. WHAT DO YOU THINK?
SURE!
COME TO THIS RINK TOMORROW AND WE'LL GET STARTED RIGHT AWAY.

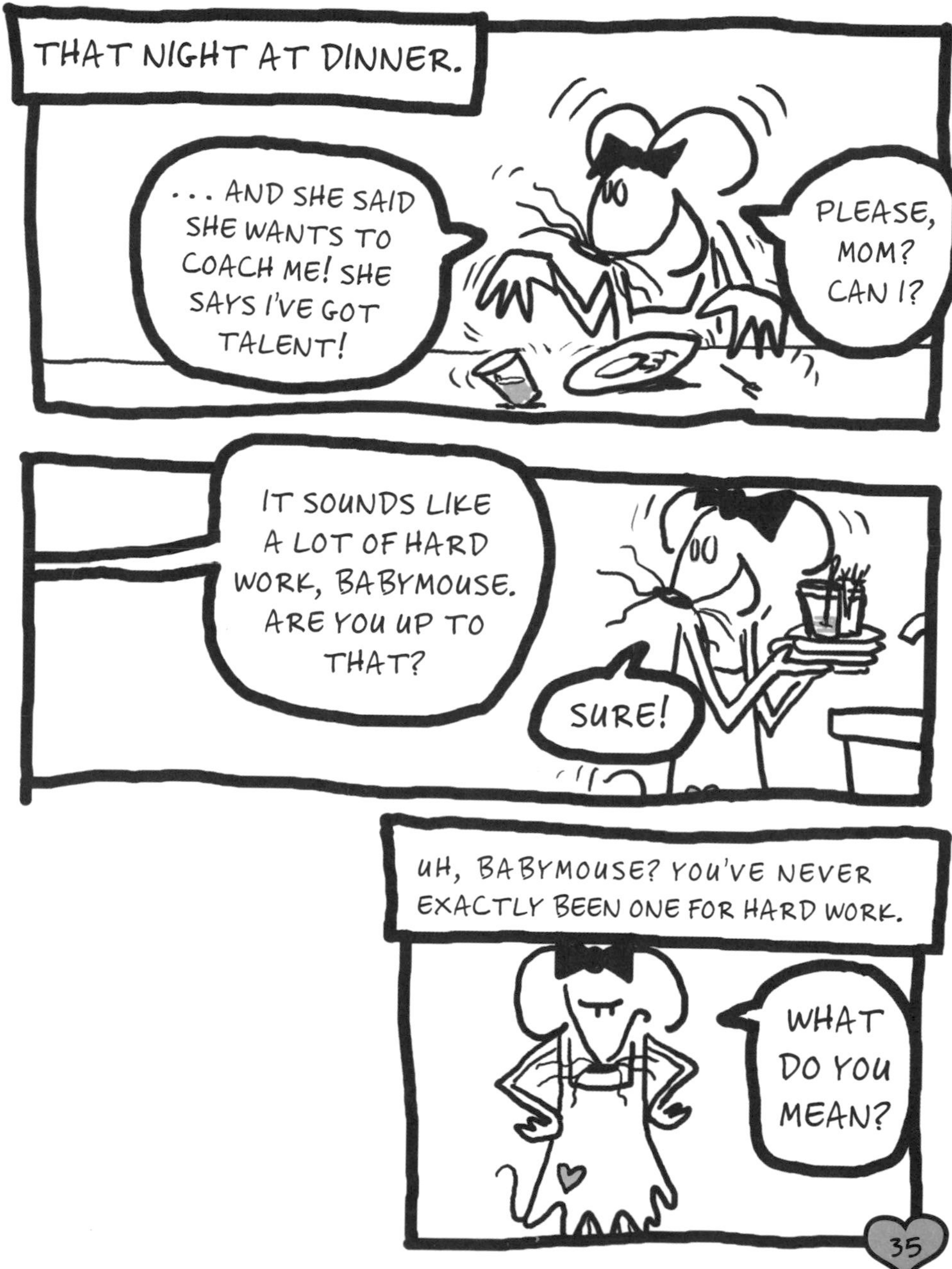
THAT NIGHT AT DINNER.
. . . AND SHE SAID SHE WANTS TO COACH ME! SHE SAYS I'VE GOT TALENT!
PLEASE, MOM? CAN I?
IT SOUNDS LIKE A LOT OF HARD WORK, BABYMOUSE. ARE YOU UP TO THAT?
SURE!
UH, BABYMOUSE? YOU'VE NEVER EXACTLY BEEN ONE FOR HARD WORK.
WHAT DO YOU MEAN?

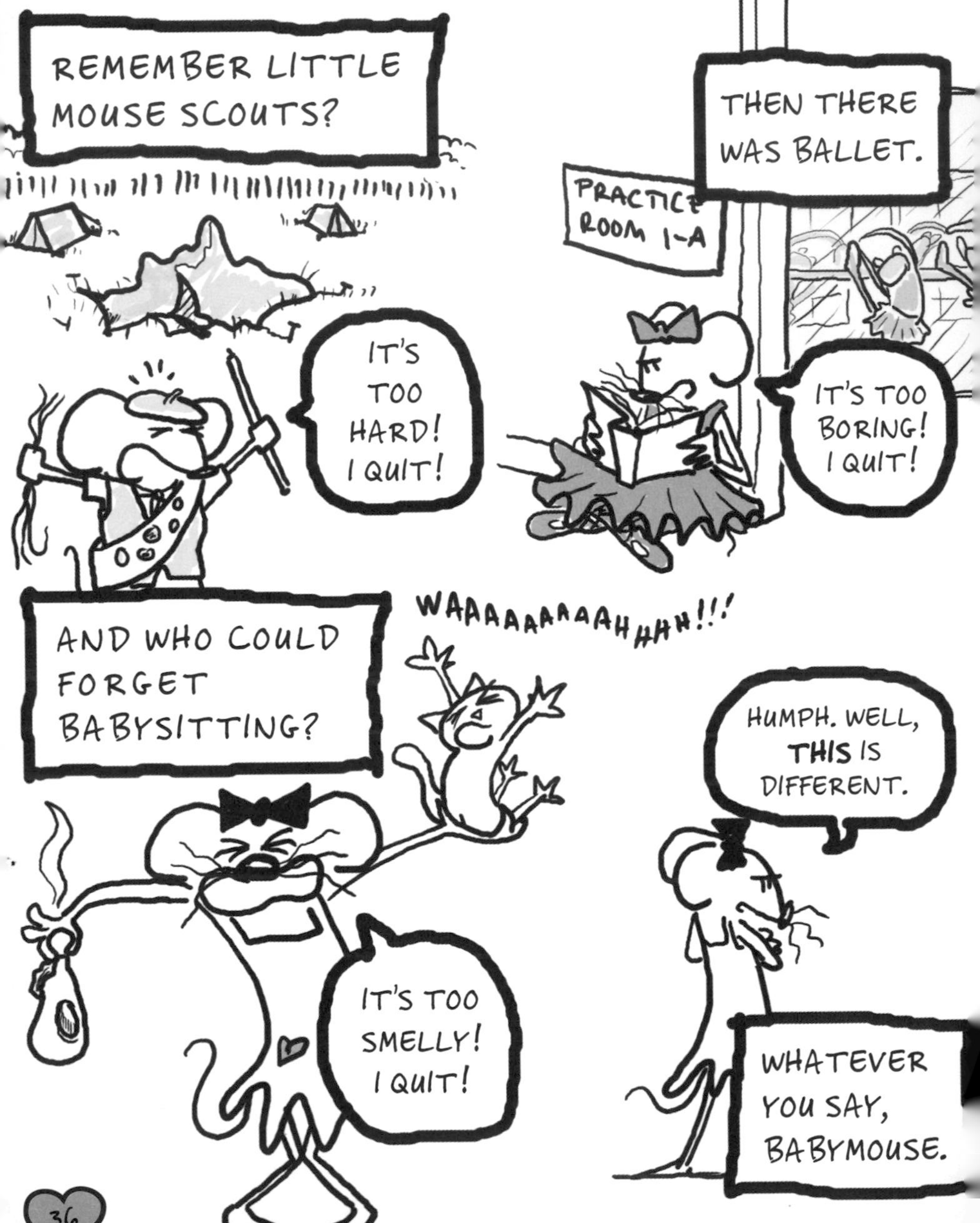
REMEMBER LITTLE MOUSE SCOUTS?
IT'S TOO HARD! I QUIT!
THEN THERE WAS BALLET.
PRACTICE ROOM 1-A
IT'S TOO BORING! I QUIT!
AND WHO COULD FORGET BABYSITTING?
WAAAAAAAAAHHHH!!!
IT'S TOO SMELLY! I QUIT!
HUMPH. WELL, **THIS** IS DIFFERENT.
WHATEVER YOU SAY, BABYMOUSE.

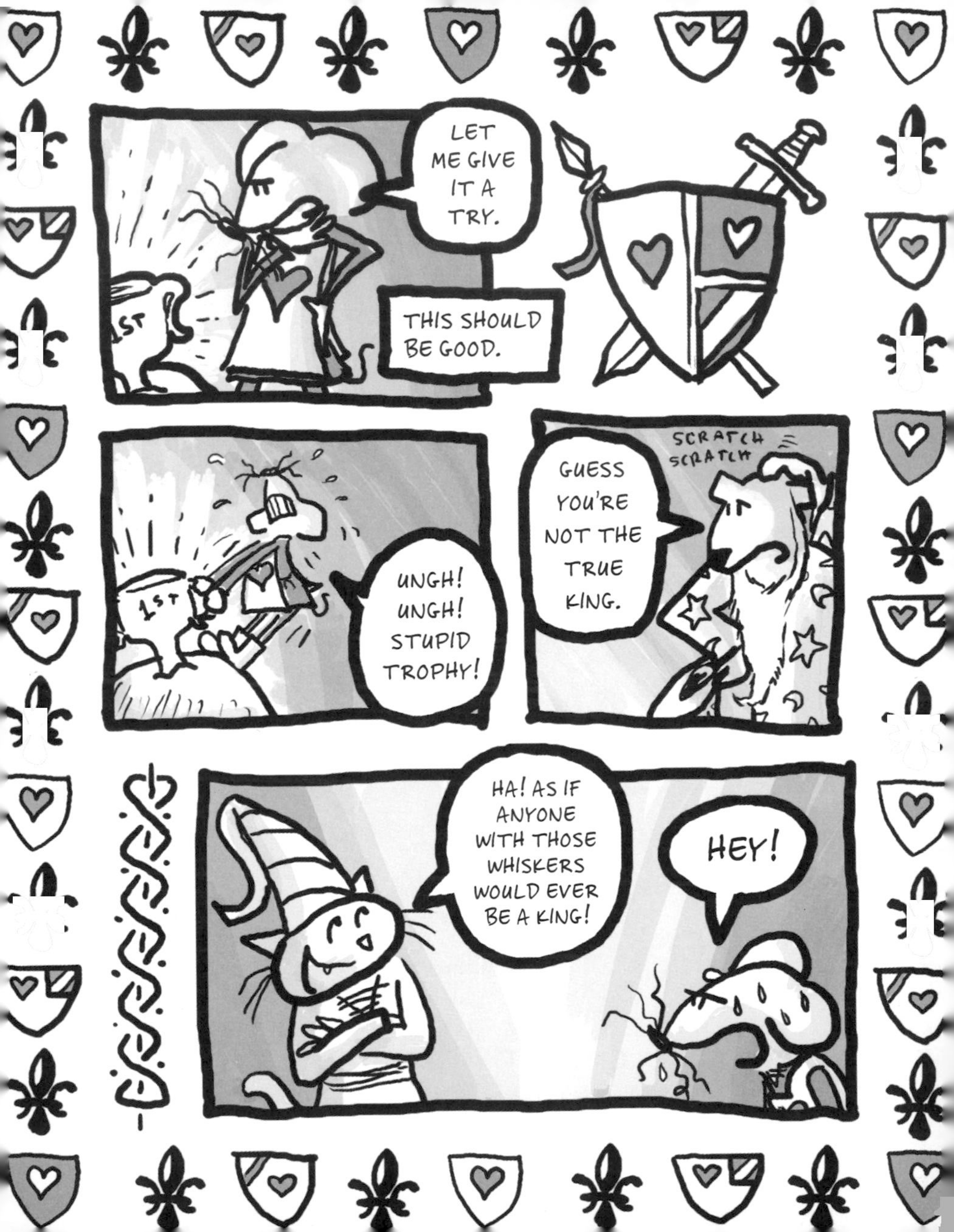
LET ME GIVE IT A TRY.
THIS SHOULD BE GOOD.
1ST
UNGH! UNGH! STUPID TROPHY!
1ST
SCRATCH SCRATCH
GUESS YOU'RE NOT THE TRUE KING.
HA! AS IF ANYONE WITH THOSE WHISKERS WOULD EVER BE A KING!
HEY!

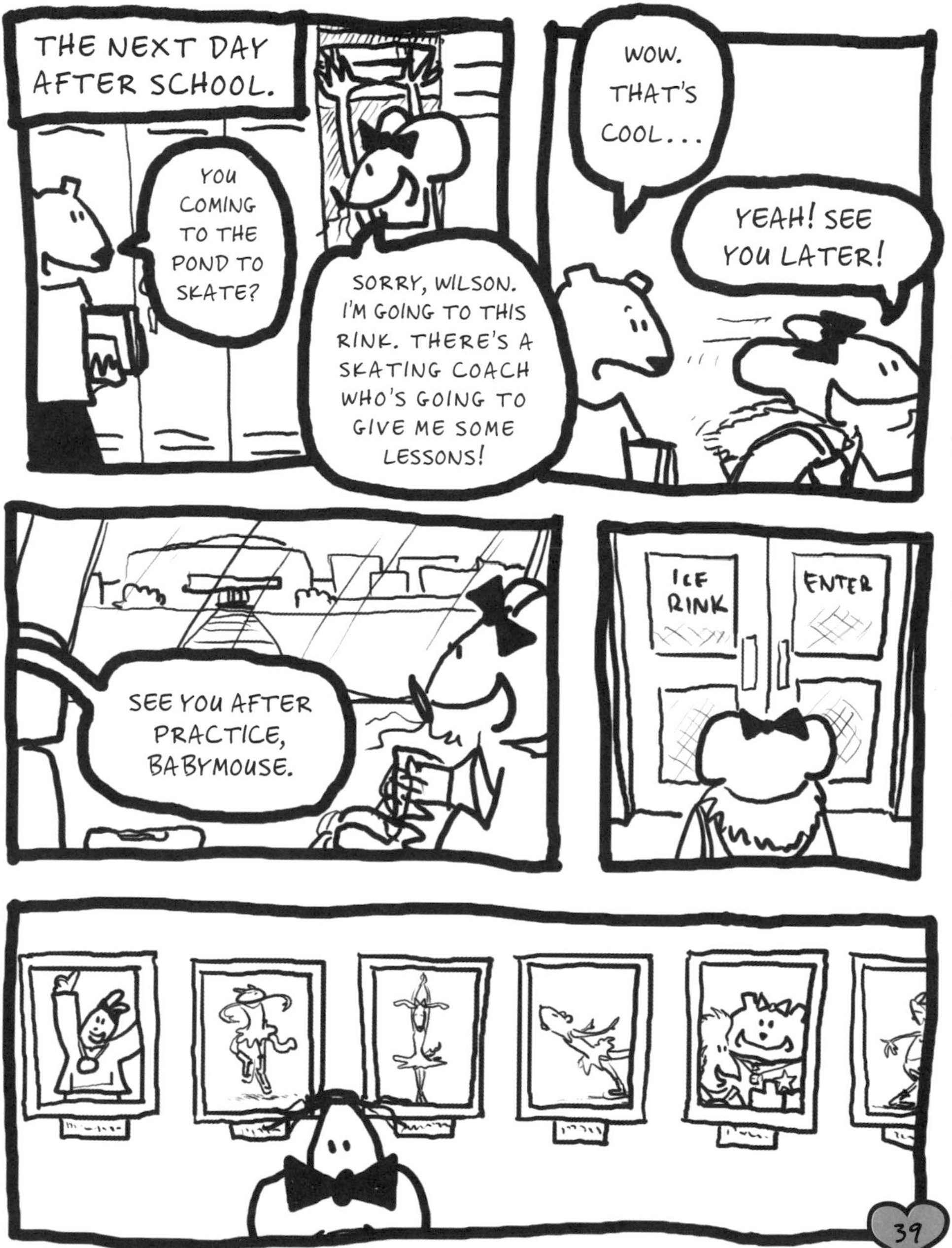
THE NEXT DAY AFTER SCHOOL.
YOU COMING TO THE POND TO SKATE?
SORRY, WILSON. I'M GOING TO THIS RINK. THERE'S A SKATING COACH WHO'S GOING TO GIVE ME SOME LESSONS!
WOW. THAT'S COOL...
YEAH! SEE YOU LATER!
SEE YOU AFTER PRACTICE, BABYMOUSE.
ICE RINK
ENTER

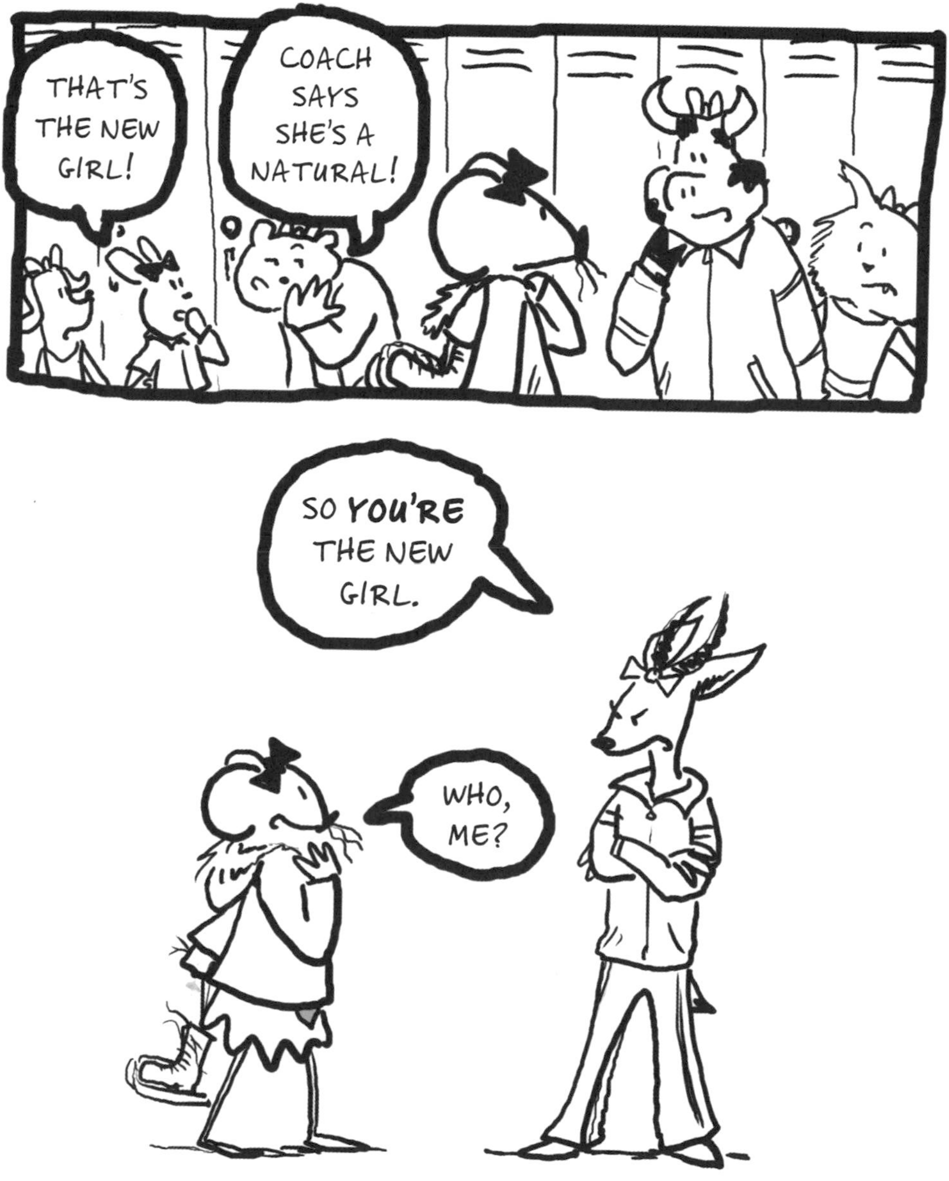
THAT'S THE NEW GIRL!
COACH SAYS SHE'S A NATURAL!
SO **YOU'RE** THE NEW GIRL.
WHO, ME?

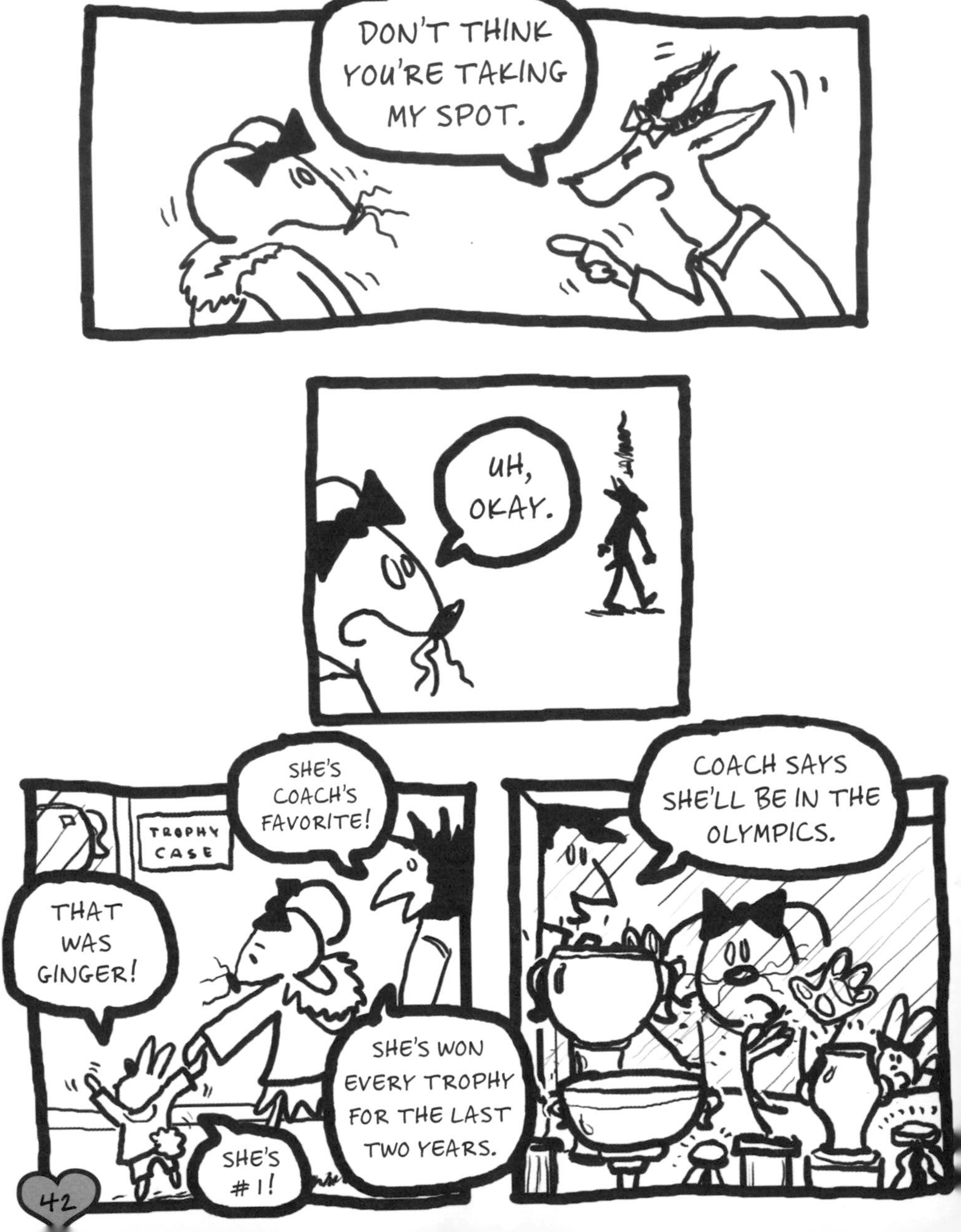
DON'T THINK YOU'RE TAKING MY SPOT.
UH, OKAY.
THAT WAS GINGER!
SHE'S COACH'S FAVORITE!
SHE'S WON EVERY TROPHY FOR THE LAST TWO YEARS.
SHE'S #1!
TROPHY CASE
COACH SAYS SHE'LL BE IN THE OLYMPICS.

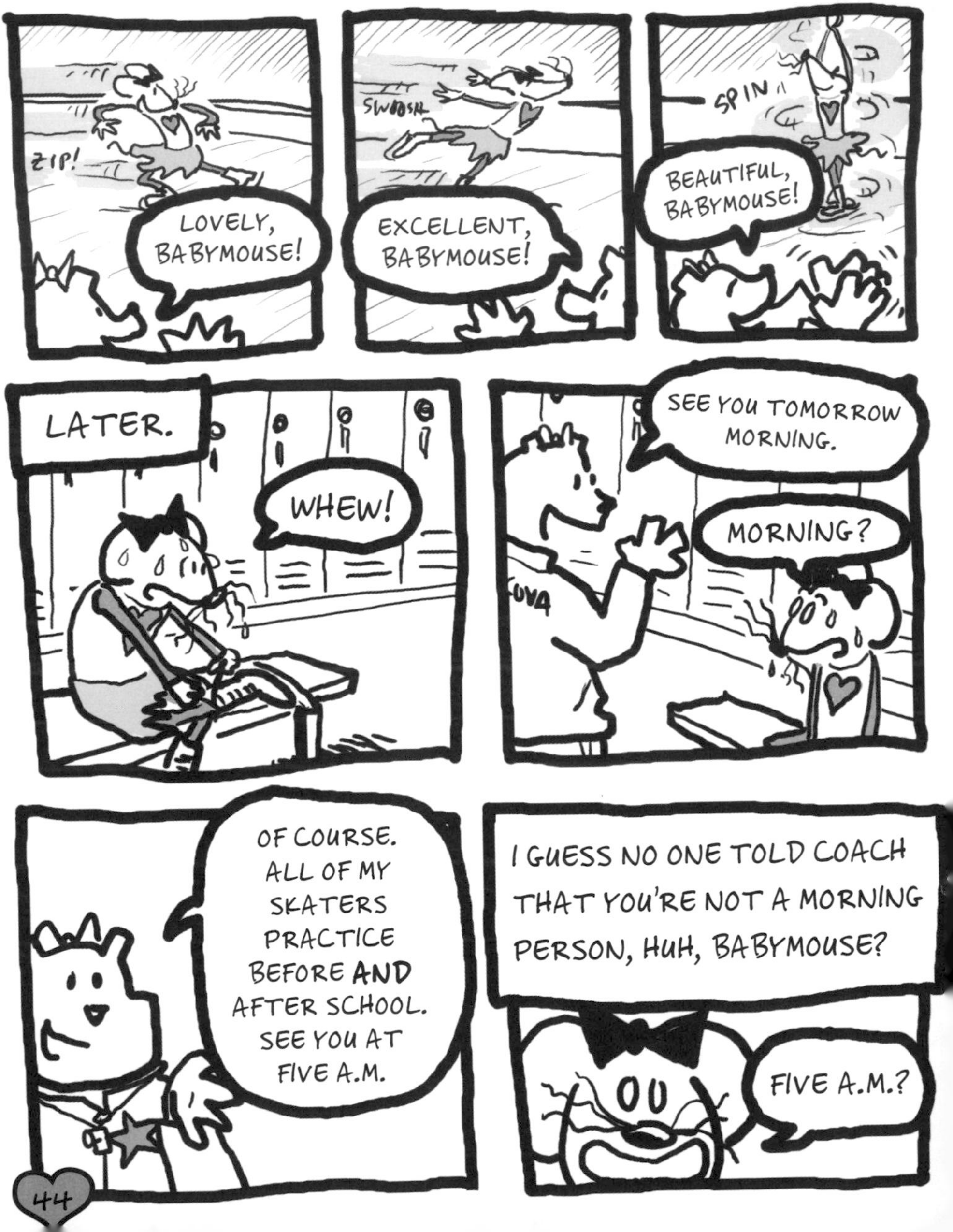
ZIP!
LOVELY, BABYMOUSE!
SWOOSH
EXCELLENT, BABYMOUSE!
SPIN
BEAUTIFUL, BABYMOUSE!
LATER.
WHEW!
SEE YOU TOMORROW MORNING.
MORNING?
OF COURSE. ALL OF MY SKATERS PRACTICE BEFORE **AND** AFTER SCHOOL. SEE YOU AT FIVE A.M.
I GUESS NO ONE TOLD COACH THAT YOU'RE NOT A MORNING PERSON, HUH, BABYMOUSE?
FIVE A.M.?

46

4:55 A.M.

ICE
RIN

8:15 A.M.

ICE
RIN

8:30 A.M.

HAVE A NICE DAY AT SCHOOL, BABYMOUSE.

UGH.

BUCK UP, BABYMOUSE. JUST THINK OF THE TROPHY AS THE GOLD AT THE END OF THE RAINBOW.

EASY FOR YOU TO SAY! YOU HAVEN'T BEEN UP SINCE 4:30!

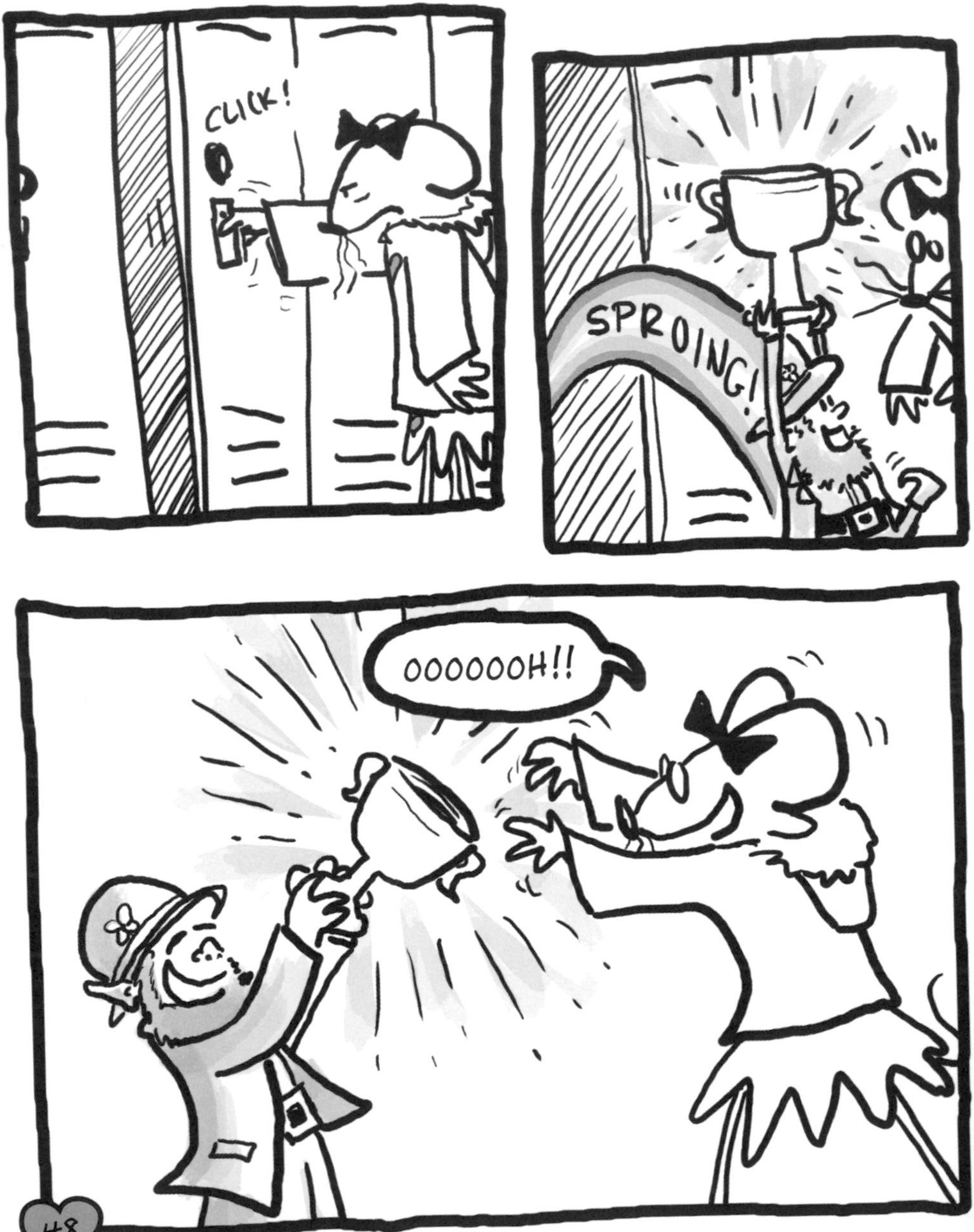
CLICK!
SPROING!
OOOOOOH!!

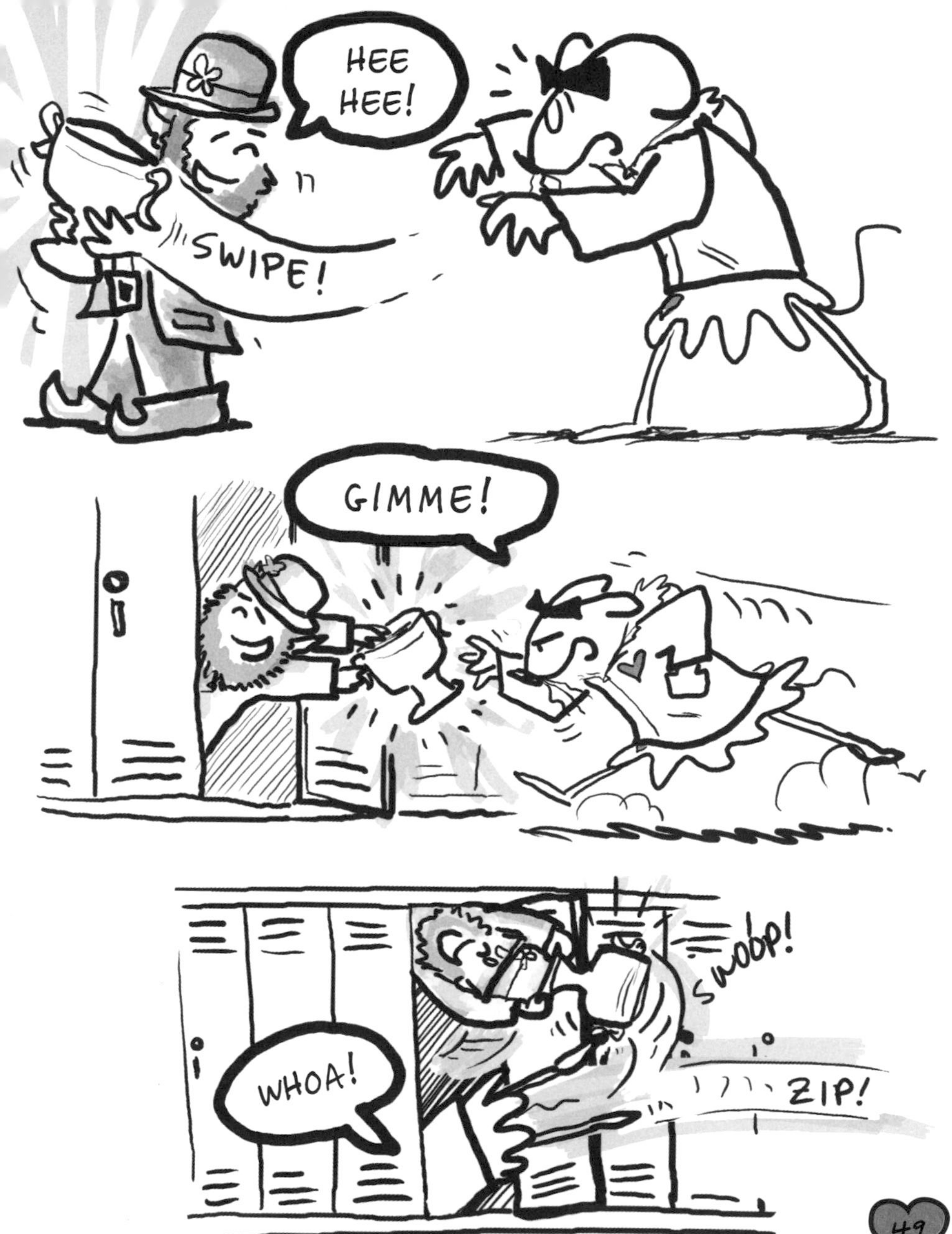
HEE HEE!
SWIPE!
GIMME!
WHOA!
SWOOP!
ZIP!

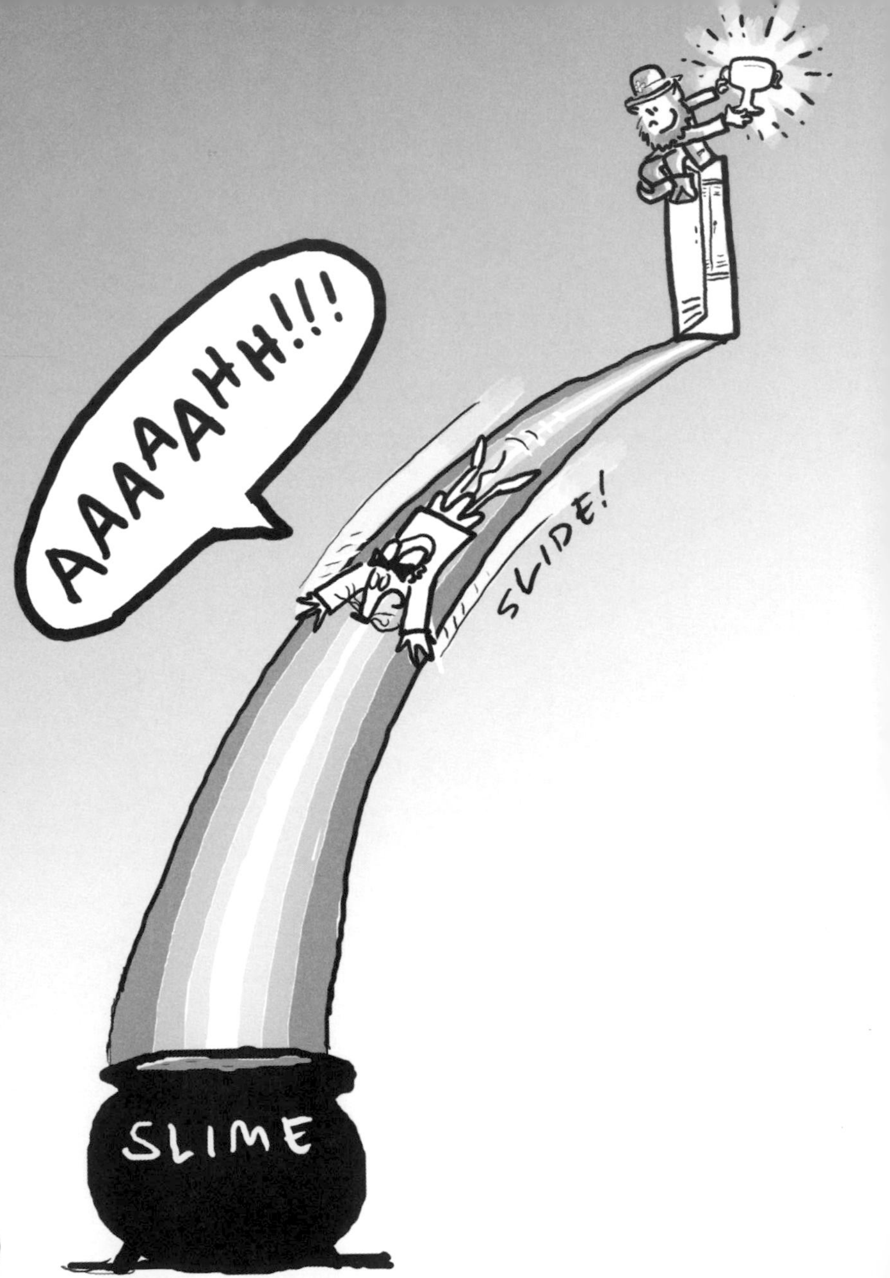
AAAAAHH!!!
SLIDE!
SLIME

51

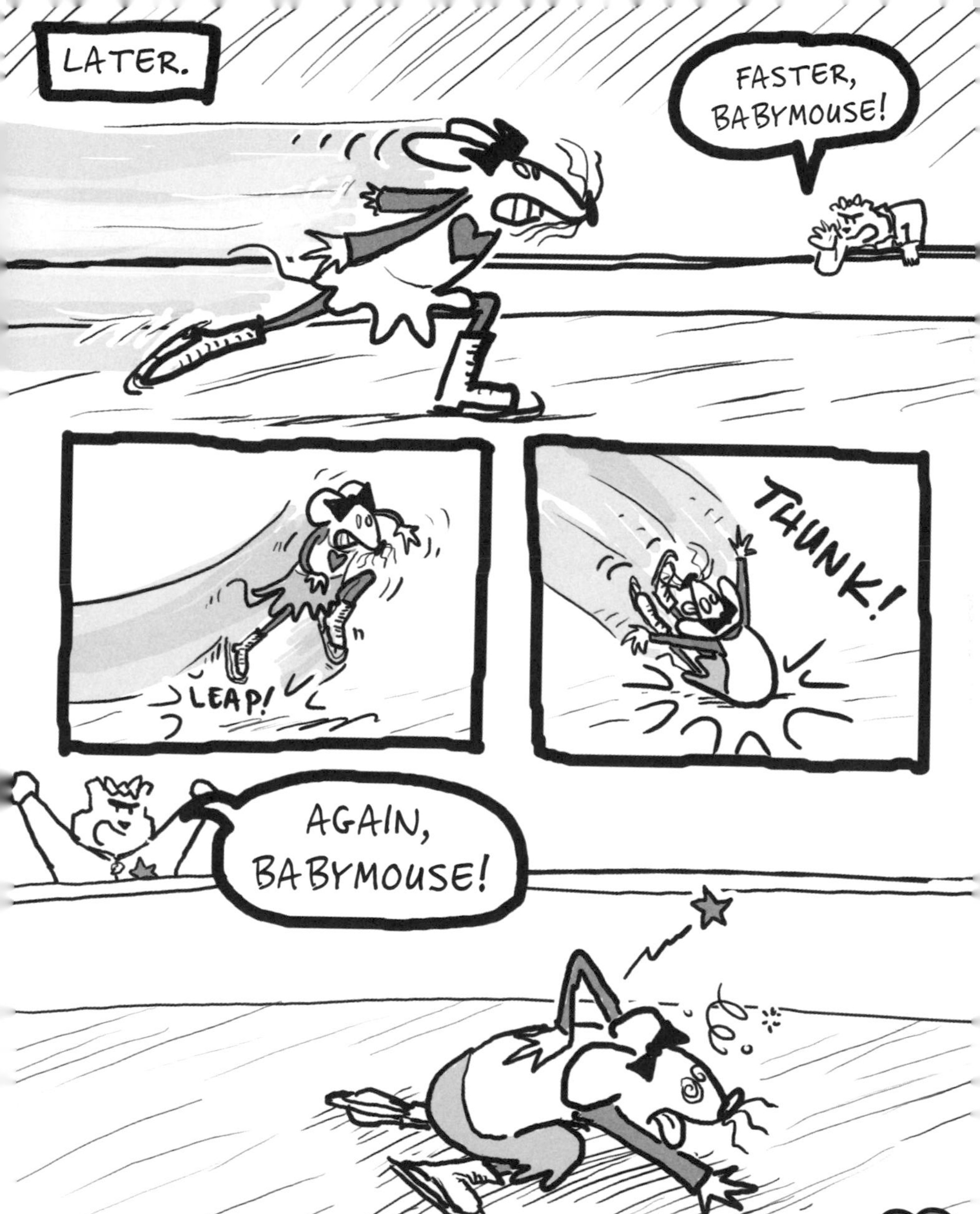
LATER.
FASTER, BABYMOUSE!
LEAP!
THUNK!
AGAIN, BABYMOUSE!

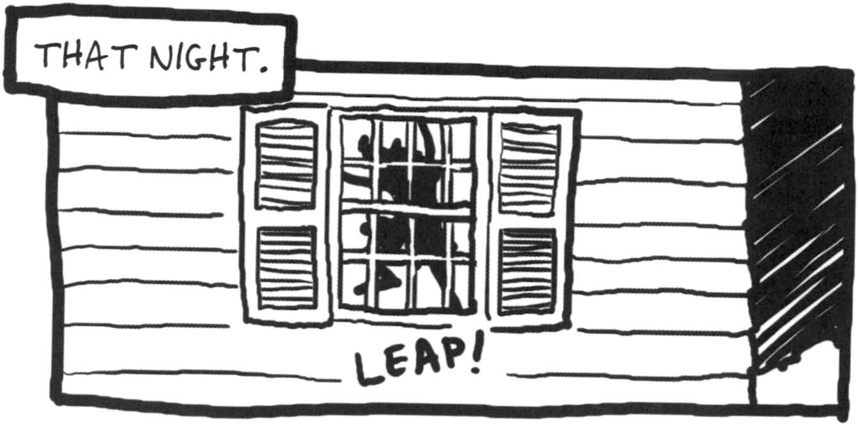
THAT NIGHT.
LEAP!

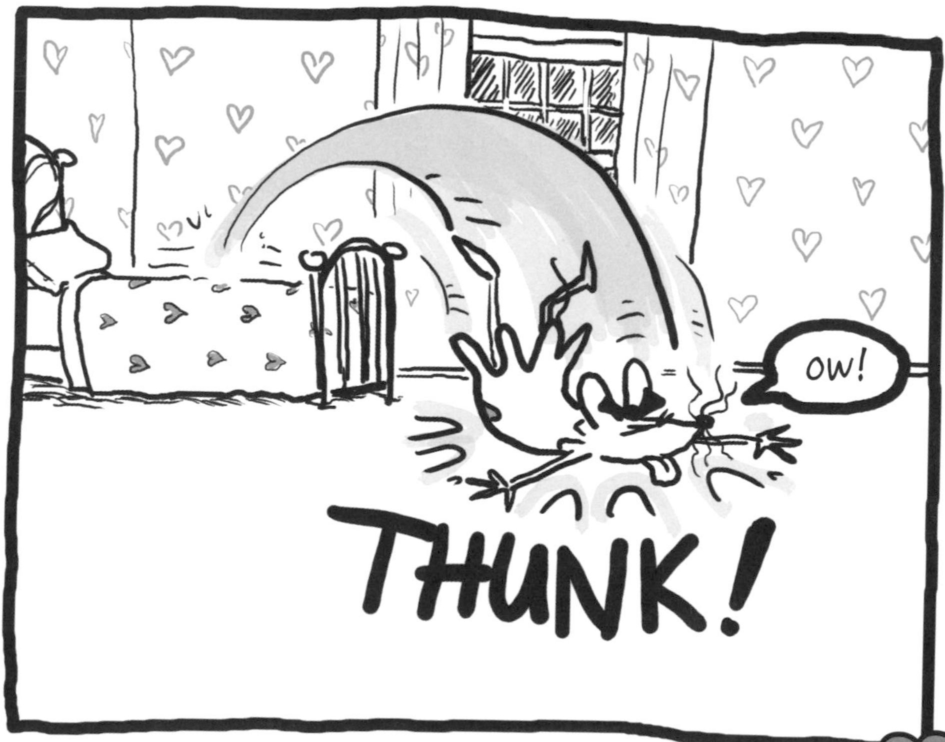
OW!
THUNK!

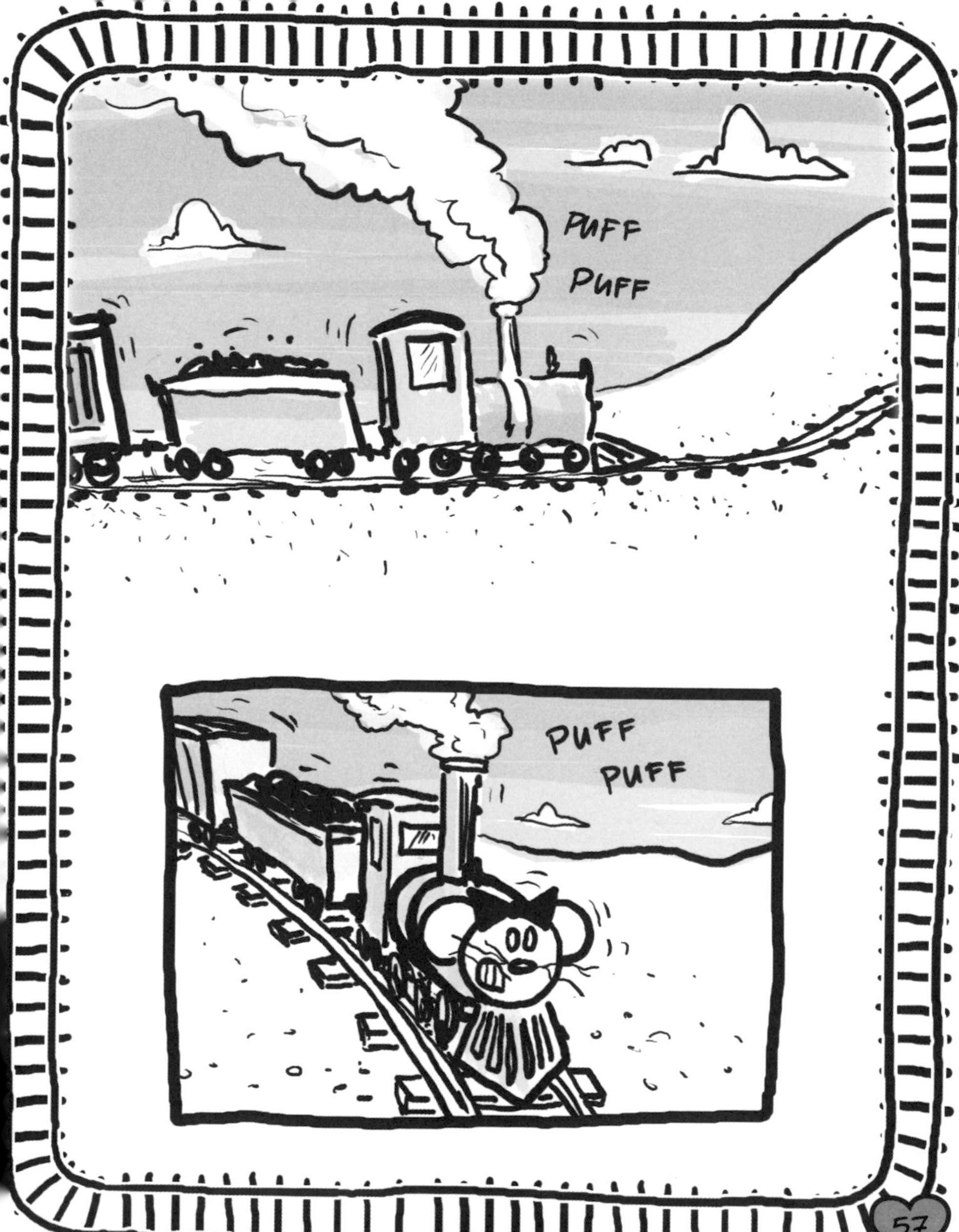
PUFF
PUFF
PUFF
PUFF

THAT'S SOME HILL, LITTLE BABYMOUSE ENGINE.

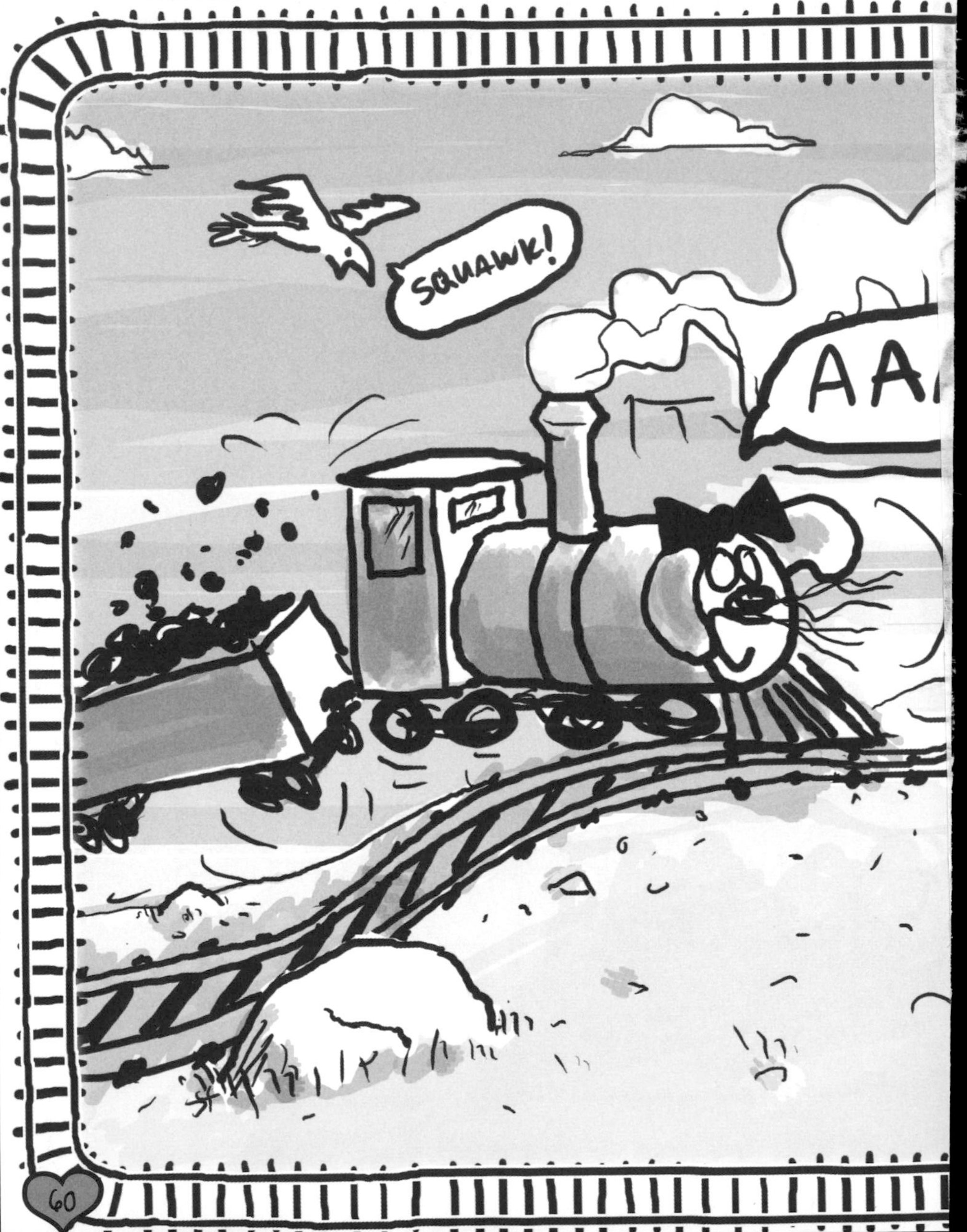
SQUAWK!
AAA

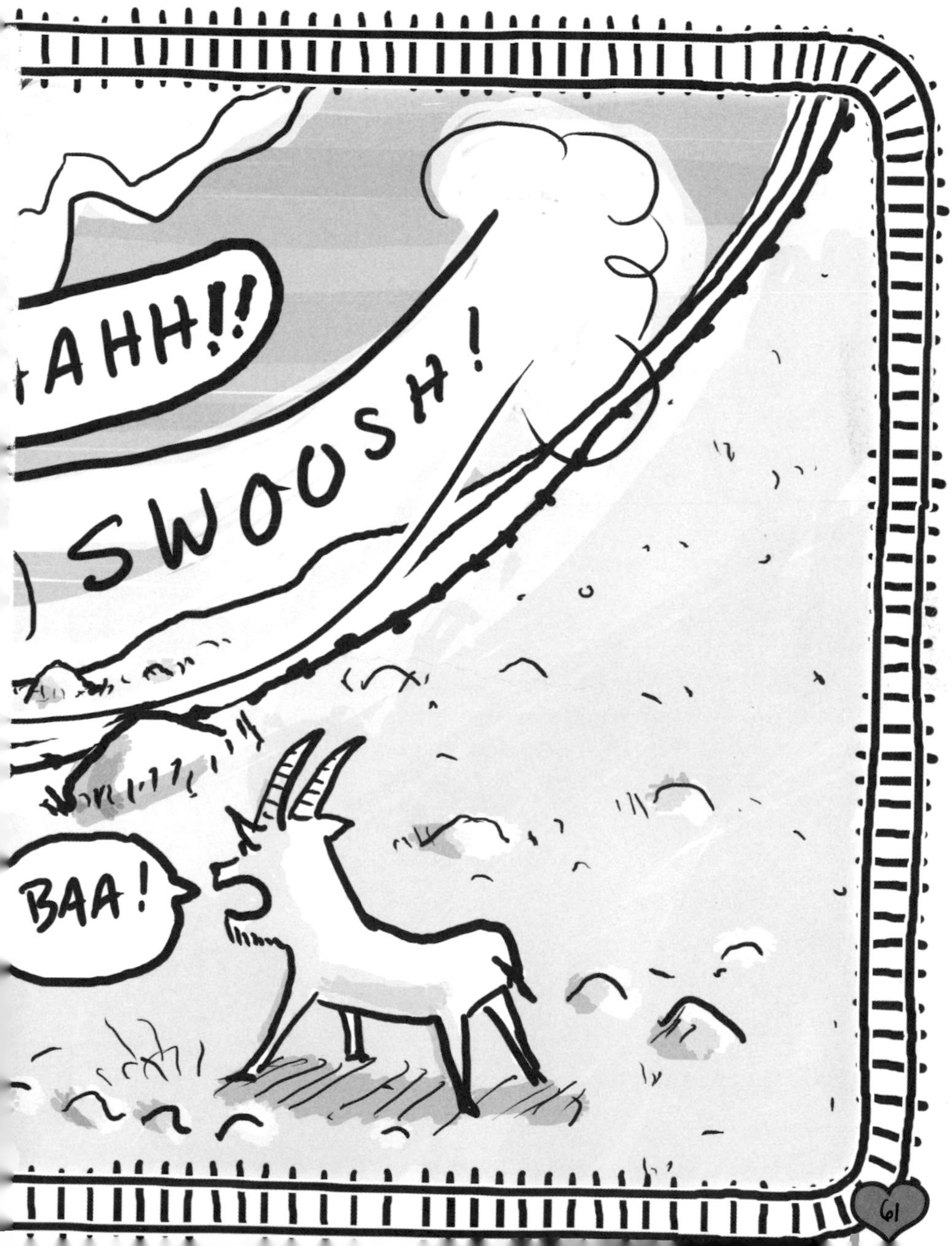
AHH!!
SWOOSH!
BAA!

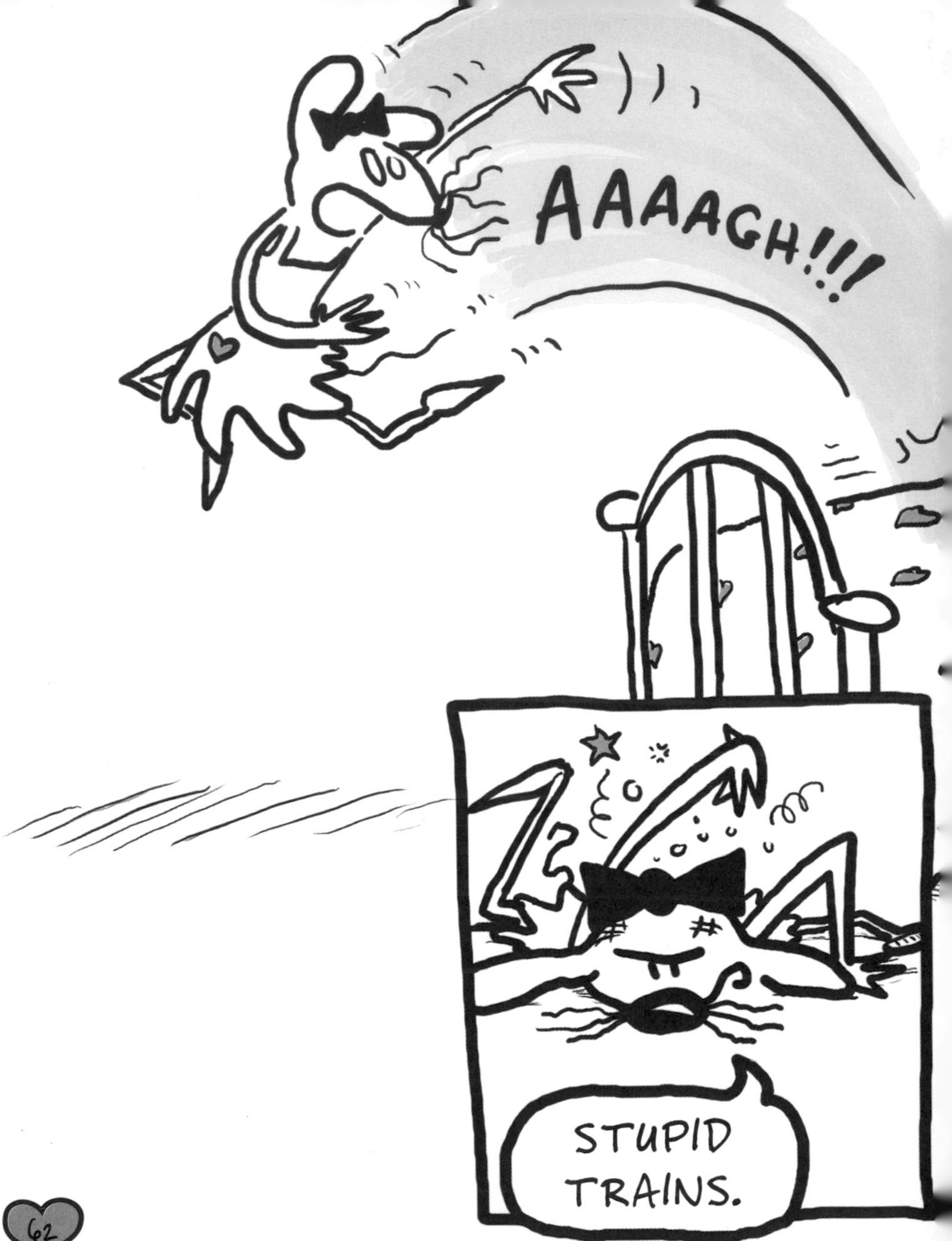
AAAAGH!!!
STUPID TRAINS.

SWOOSH!

JUMP!

SPIN

ZIP

TWIST

SWOOSH!

TWIRL

PING!

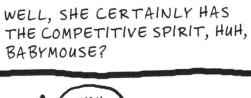

WELL, SHE CERTAINLY HAS THE COMPETITIVE SPIRIT, HUH, BABYMOUSE?

SIGH.

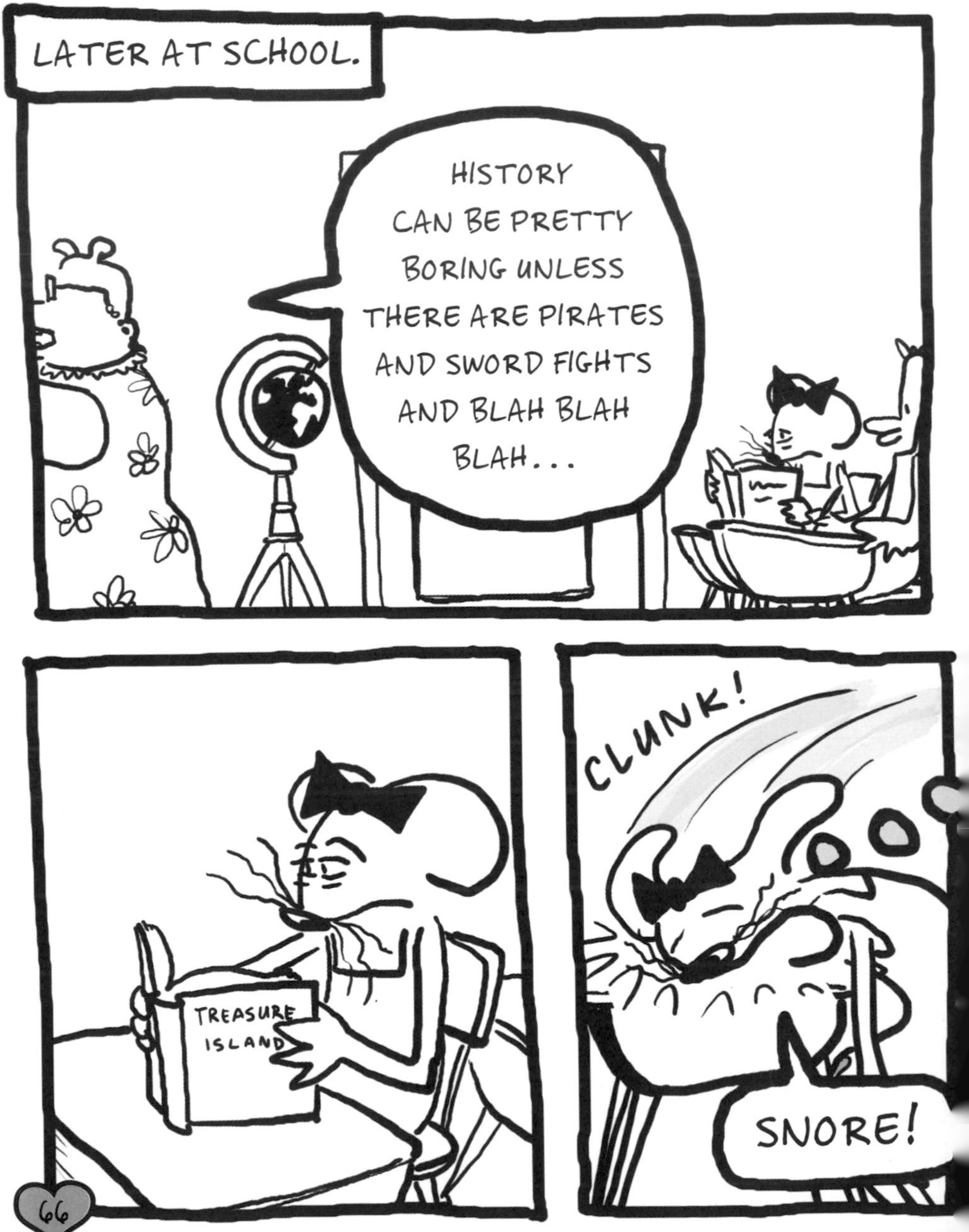
LATER AT SCHOOL.
HISTORY CAN BE PRETTY BORING UNLESS THERE ARE PIRATES AND SWORD FIGHTS AND BLAH BLAH BLAH...
TREASURE ISLAND
CLUNK!
SNORE!

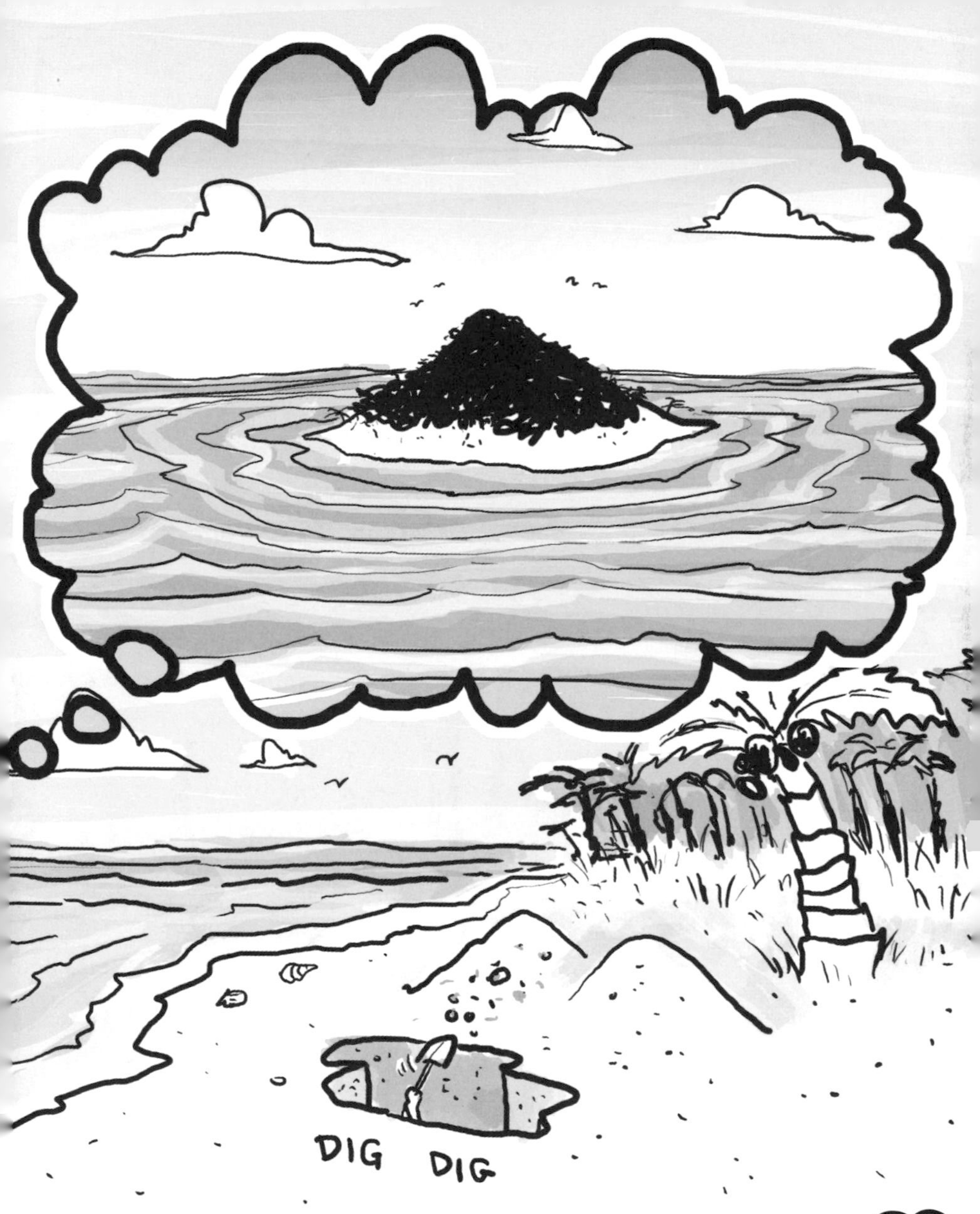
DIG DIG

THE TRAINING OF A WINNER!

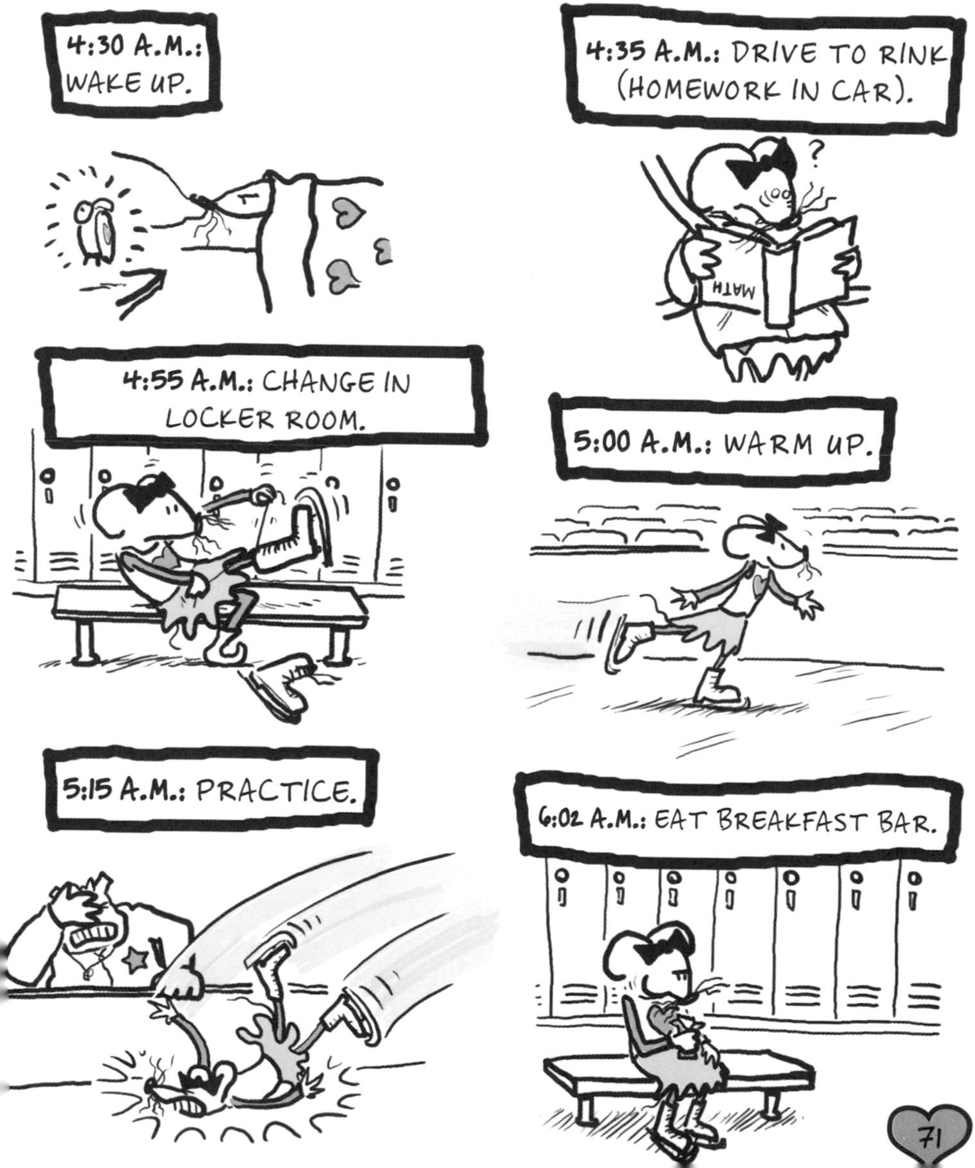
4:30 A.M.: WAKE UP.
4:35 A.M.: DRIVE TO RINK (HOMEWORK IN CAR).
?
MATH
4:55 A.M.: CHANGE IN LOCKER ROOM.
5:00 A.M.: WARM UP.
5:15 A.M.: PRACTICE.
6:02 A.M.: EAT BREAKFAST BAR.

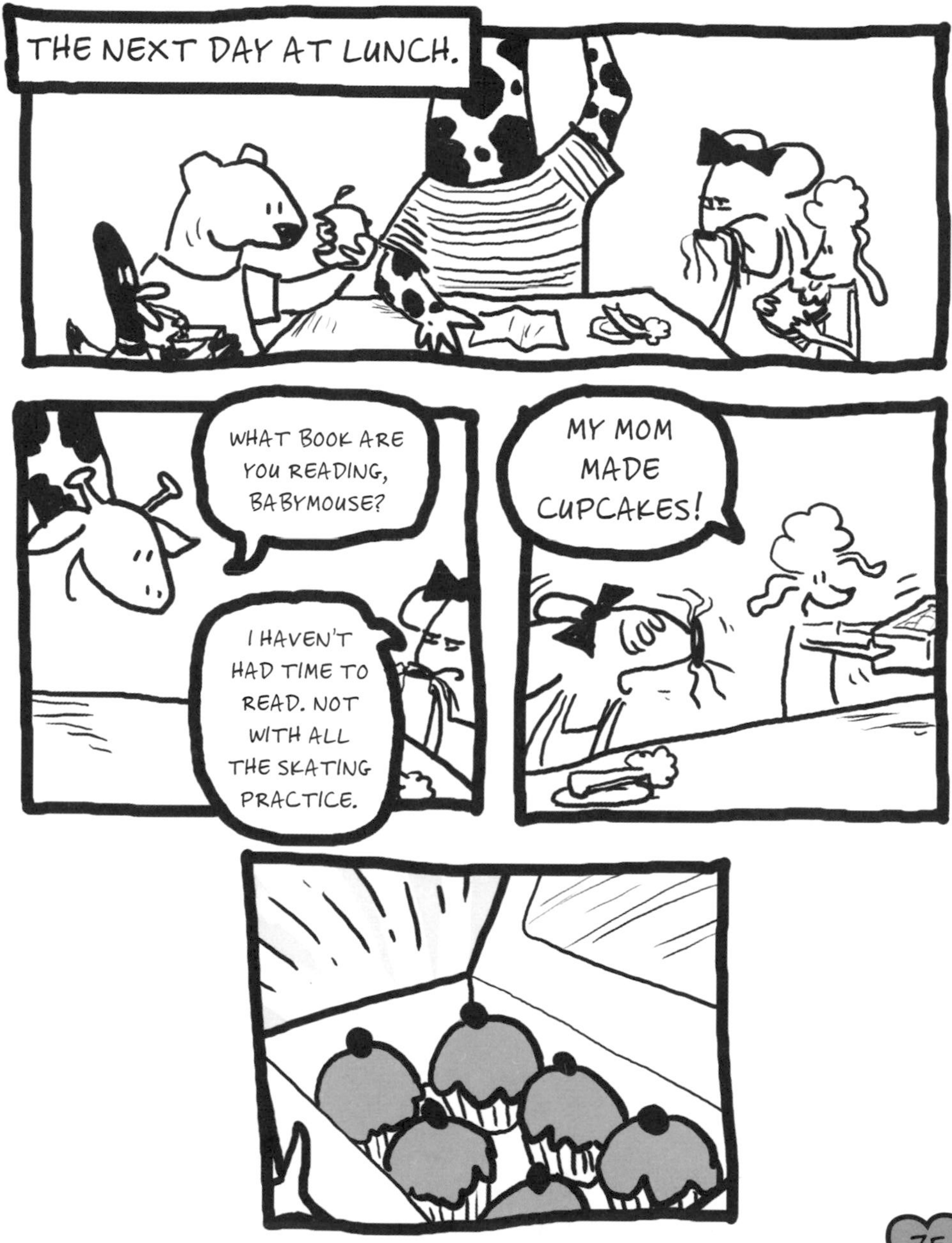
THE NEXT DAY AT LUNCH.
WHAT BOOK ARE YOU READING, BABYMOUSE?
I HAVEN'T HAD TIME TO READ. NOT WITH ALL THE SKATING PRACTICE.
MY MOM MADE CUPCAKES!

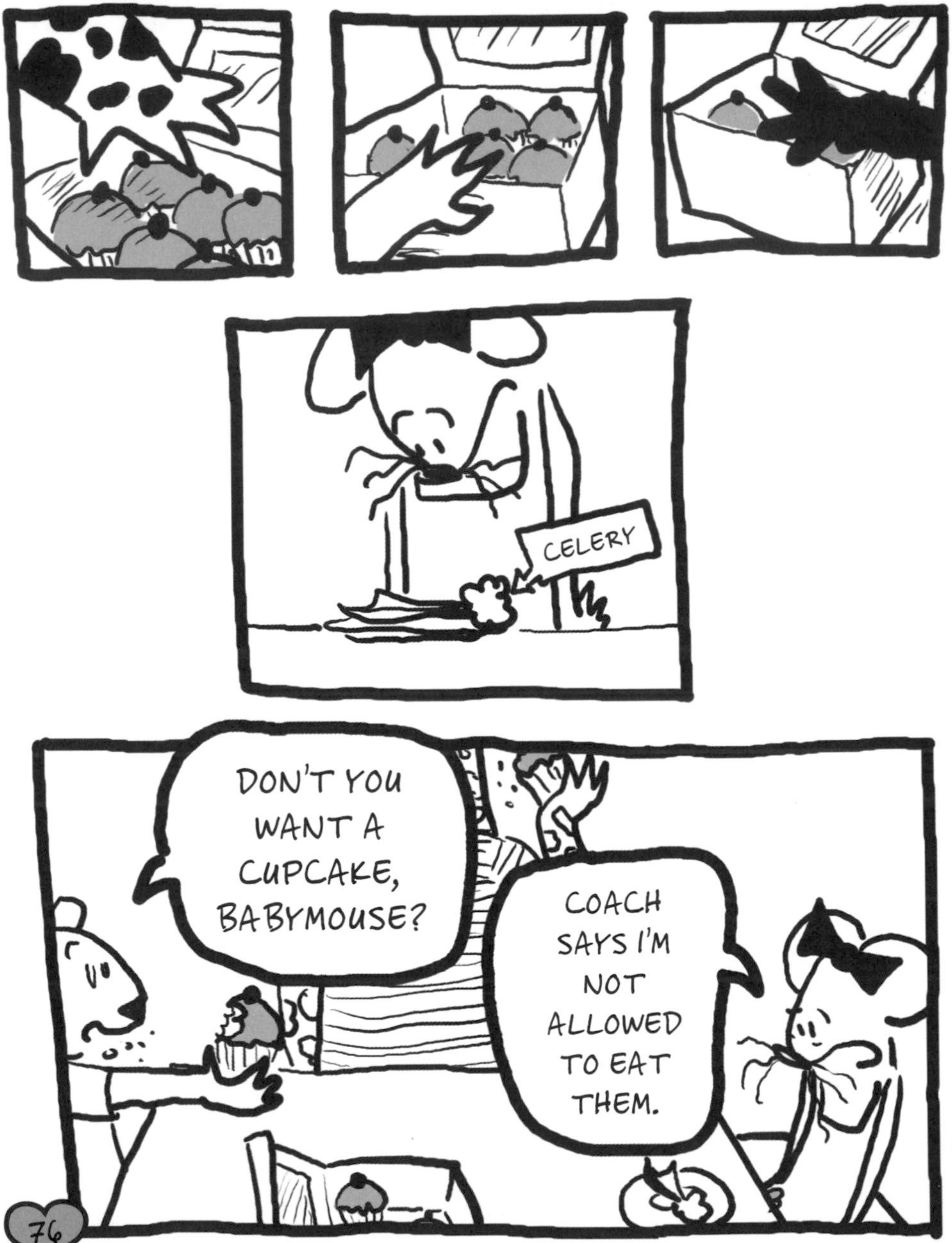
CELERY
DON'T YOU WANT A CUPCAKE, BABYMOUSE?
COACH SAYS I'M NOT ALLOWED TO EAT THEM.

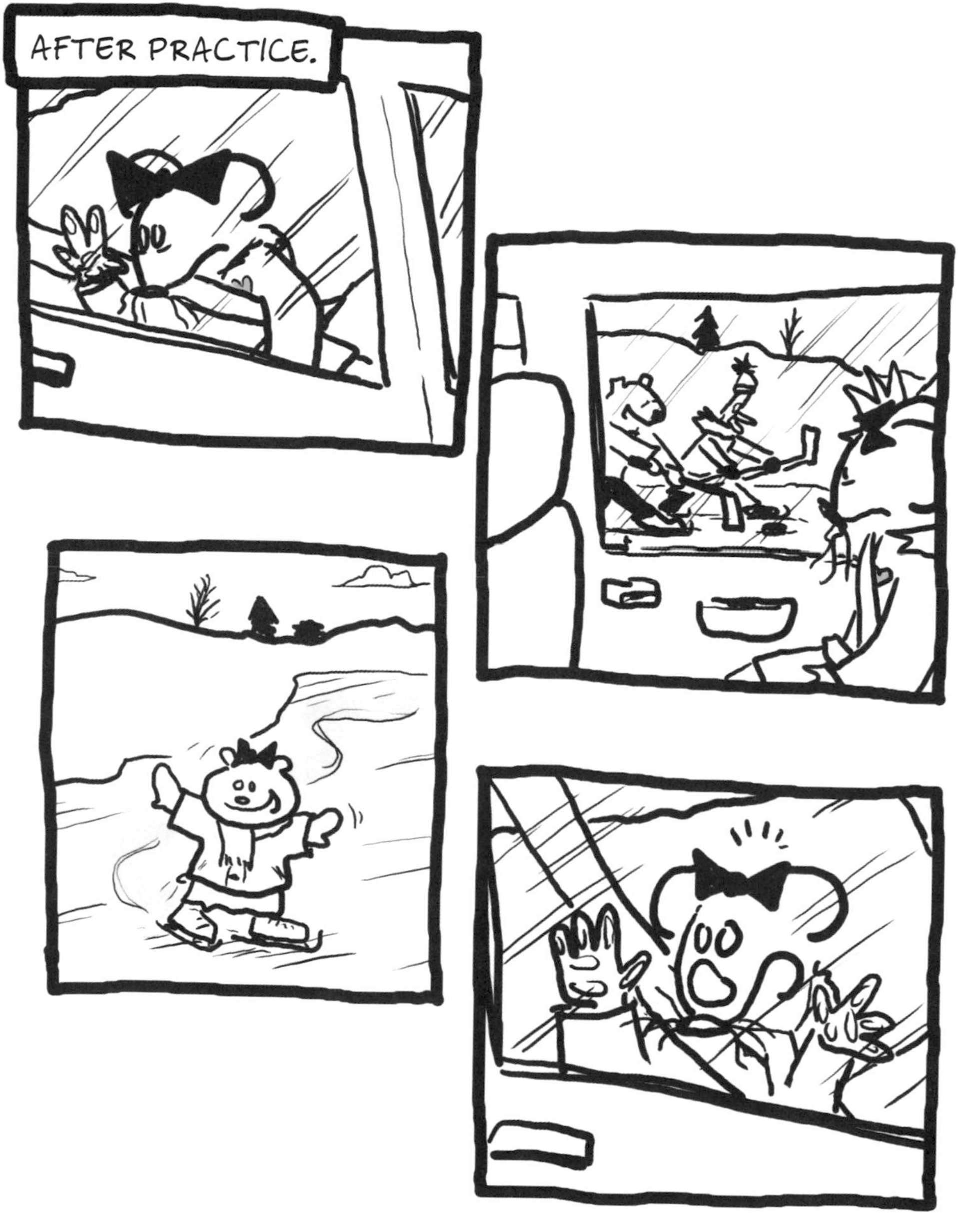
AFTER PRACTICE.

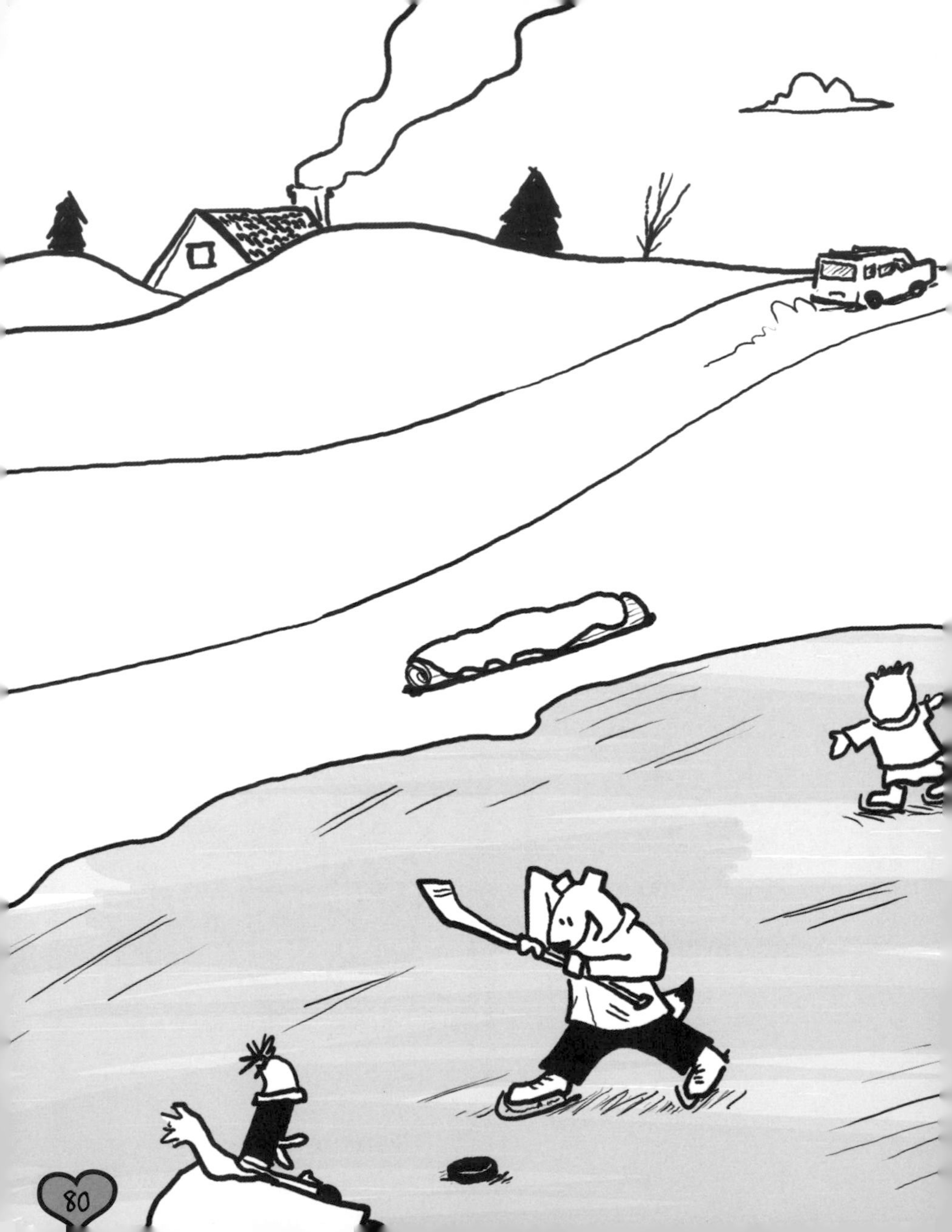

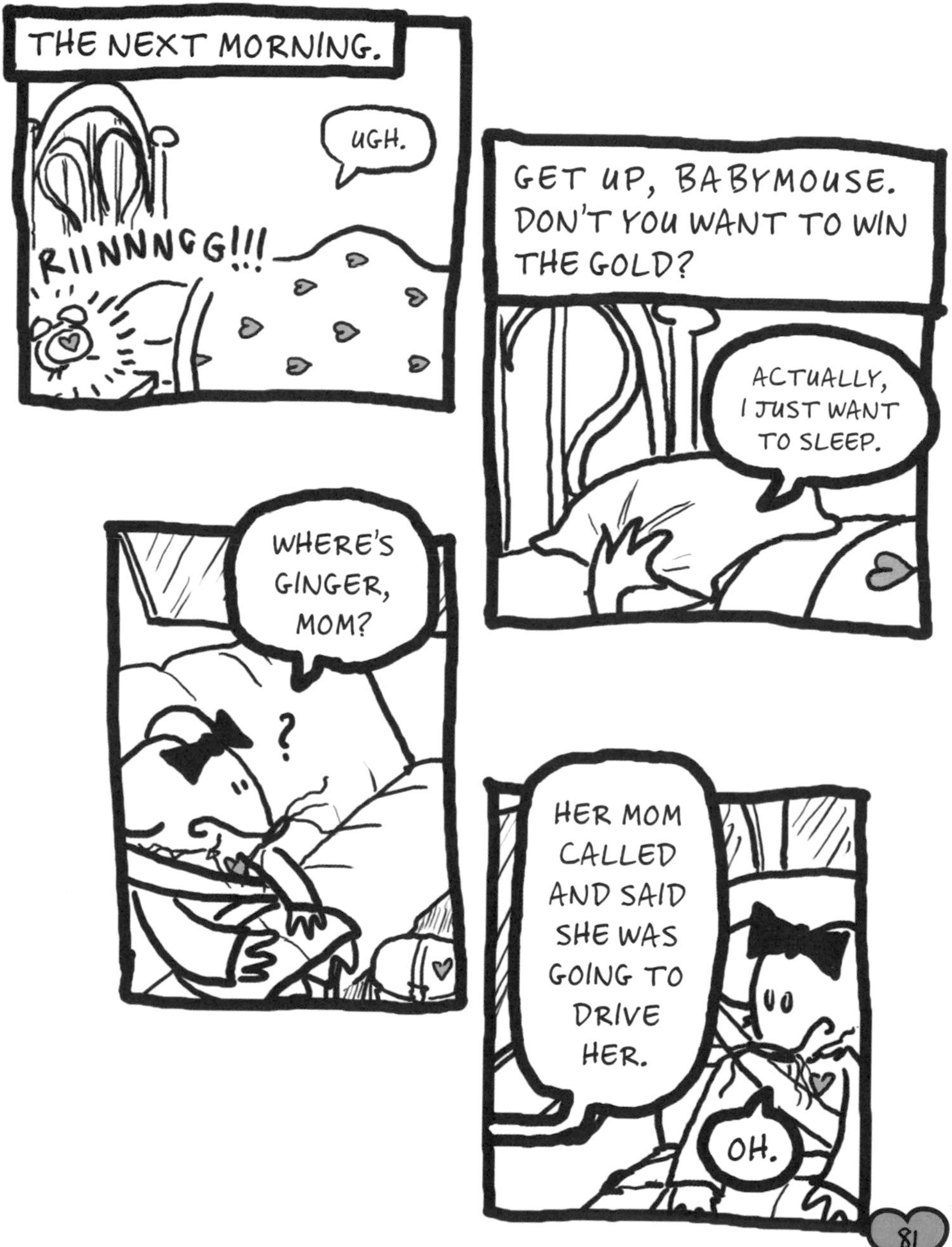
THE NEXT MORNING.
UGH.
RIINNNGG!!!
GET UP, BABYMOUSE. DON'T YOU WANT TO WIN THE GOLD?
ACTUALLY, I JUST WANT TO SLEEP.
WHERE'S GINGER, MOM?
?
HER MOM CALLED AND SAID SHE WAS GOING TO DRIVE HER.
OH.

82

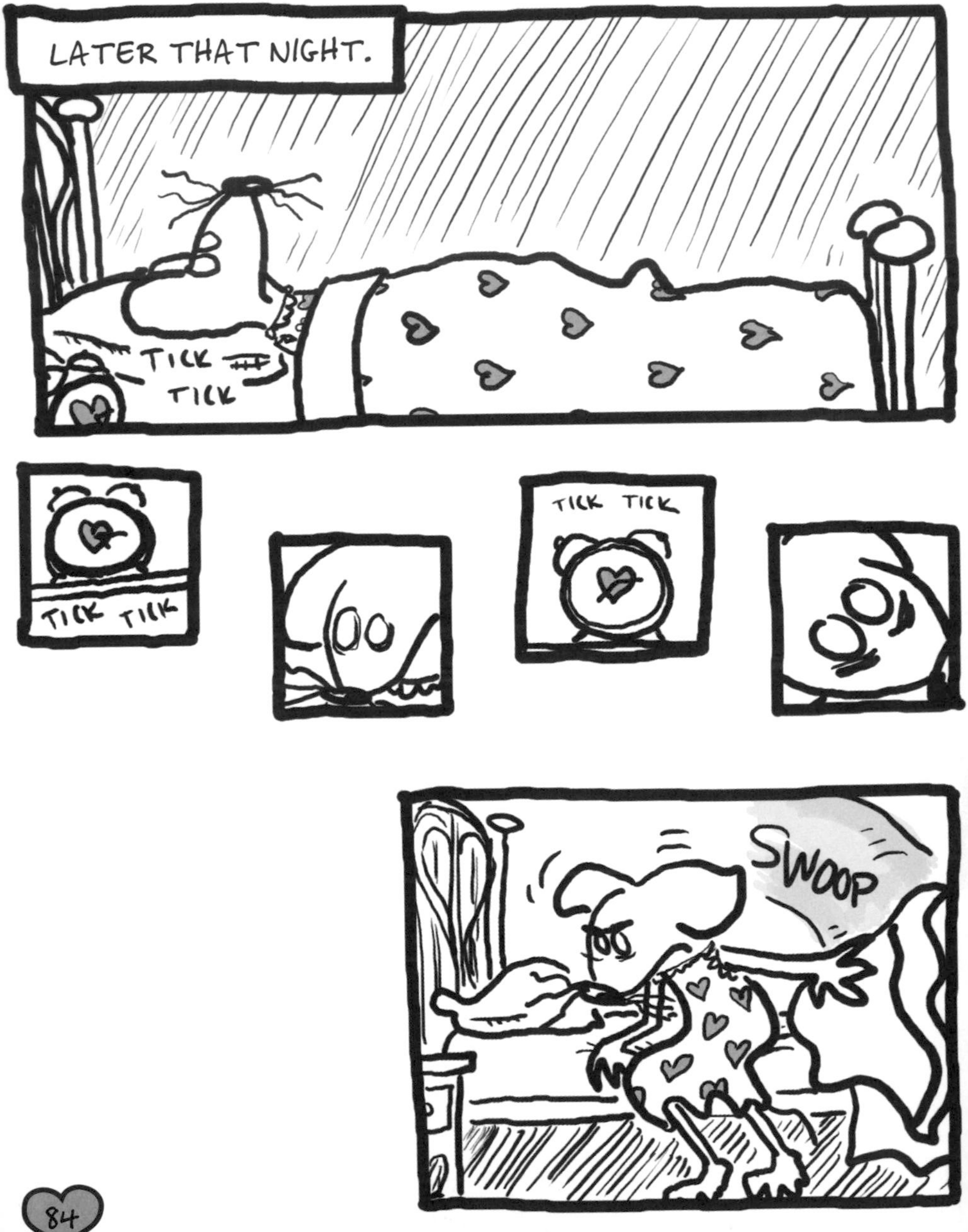
LATER THAT NIGHT.
TICK
TICK
TICK TICK
TICK TICK
SWOOP

ARE YOU SUPPOSED TO BE
EATING THAT, BABYMOUSE?

MUNCH
MUNCH

I DON'T CARE!

CREEEAK!!

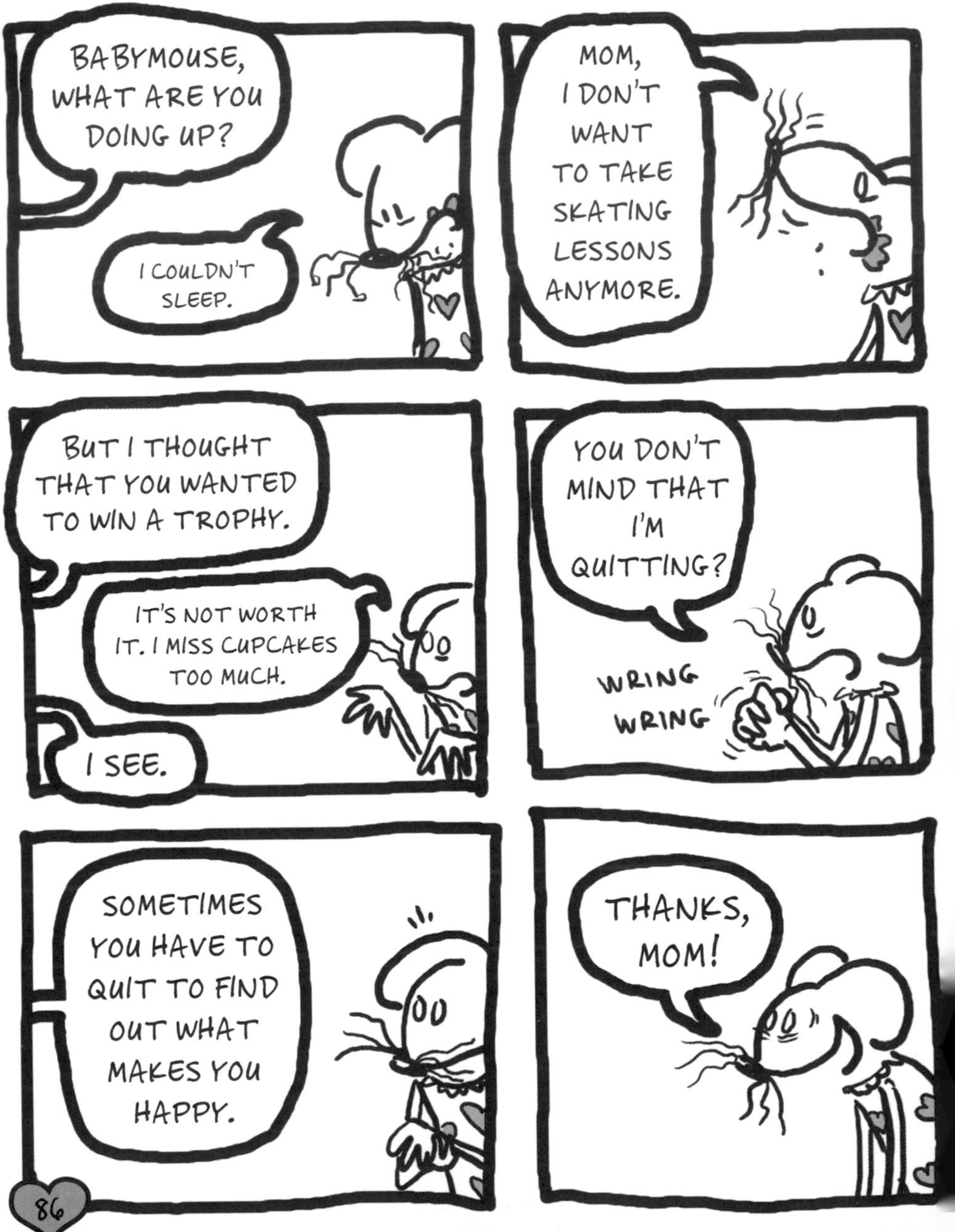
BABYMOUSE, WHAT ARE YOU DOING UP?
I COULDN'T SLEEP.
MOM, I DON'T WANT TO TAKE SKATING LESSONS ANYMORE.
BUT I THOUGHT THAT YOU WANTED TO WIN A TROPHY.
IT'S NOT WORTH IT. I MISS CUPCAKES TOO MUCH.
I SEE.
YOU DON'T MIND THAT I'M QUITTING?
WRING WRING
SOMETIMES YOU HAVE TO QUIT TO FIND OUT WHAT MAKES YOU HAPPY.
THANKS, MOM!

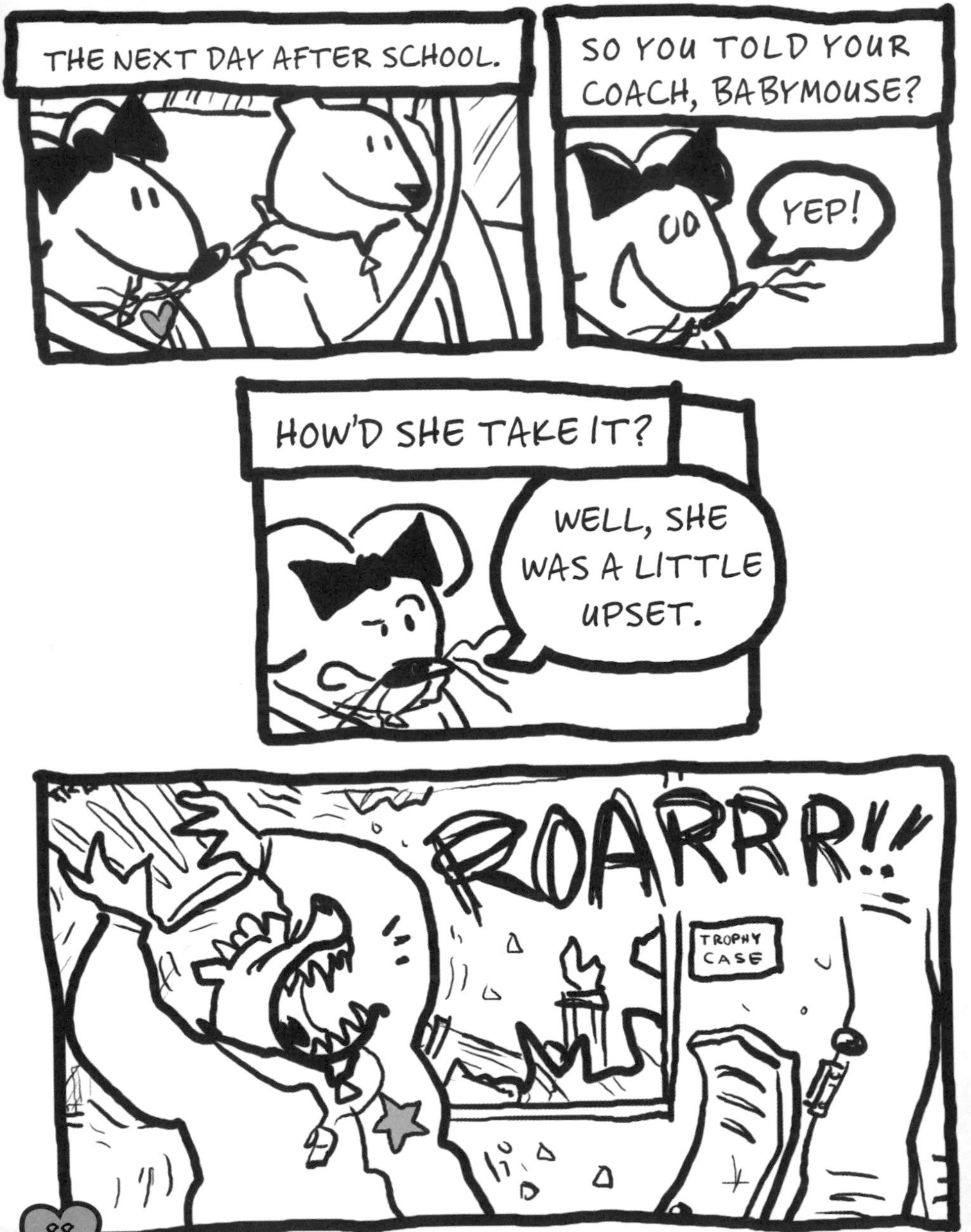
THE NEXT DAY AFTER SCHOOL.
SO YOU TOLD YOUR COACH, BABYMOUSE?
YEP!
HOW'D SHE TAKE IT?
WELL, SHE WAS A LITTLE UPSET.
ROARRRR!!
TROPHY CASE

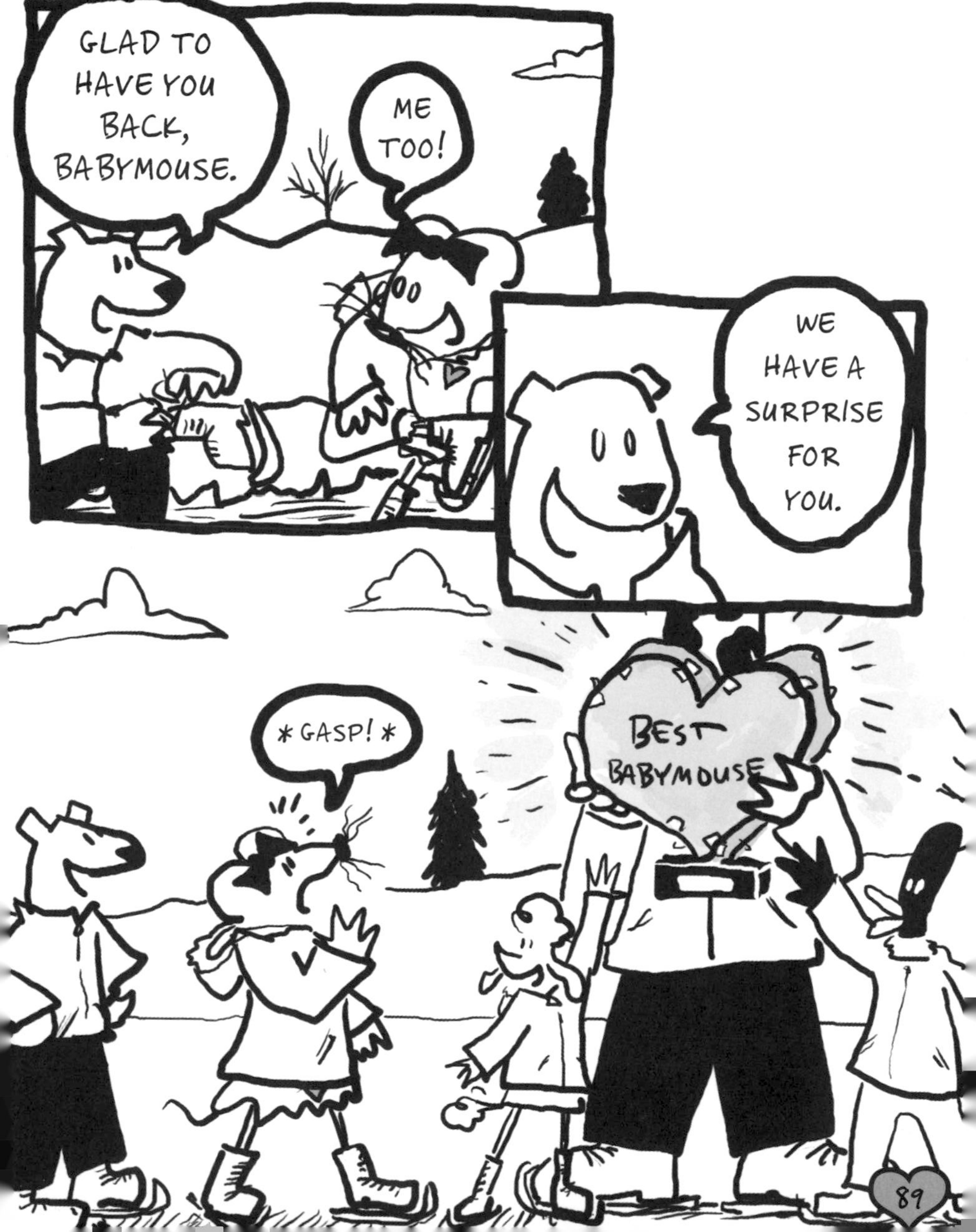
GLAD TO HAVE YOU BACK, BABYMOUSE.
ME TOO!
WE HAVE A SURPRISE FOR YOU.
GASP!
BEST BABYMOUSE

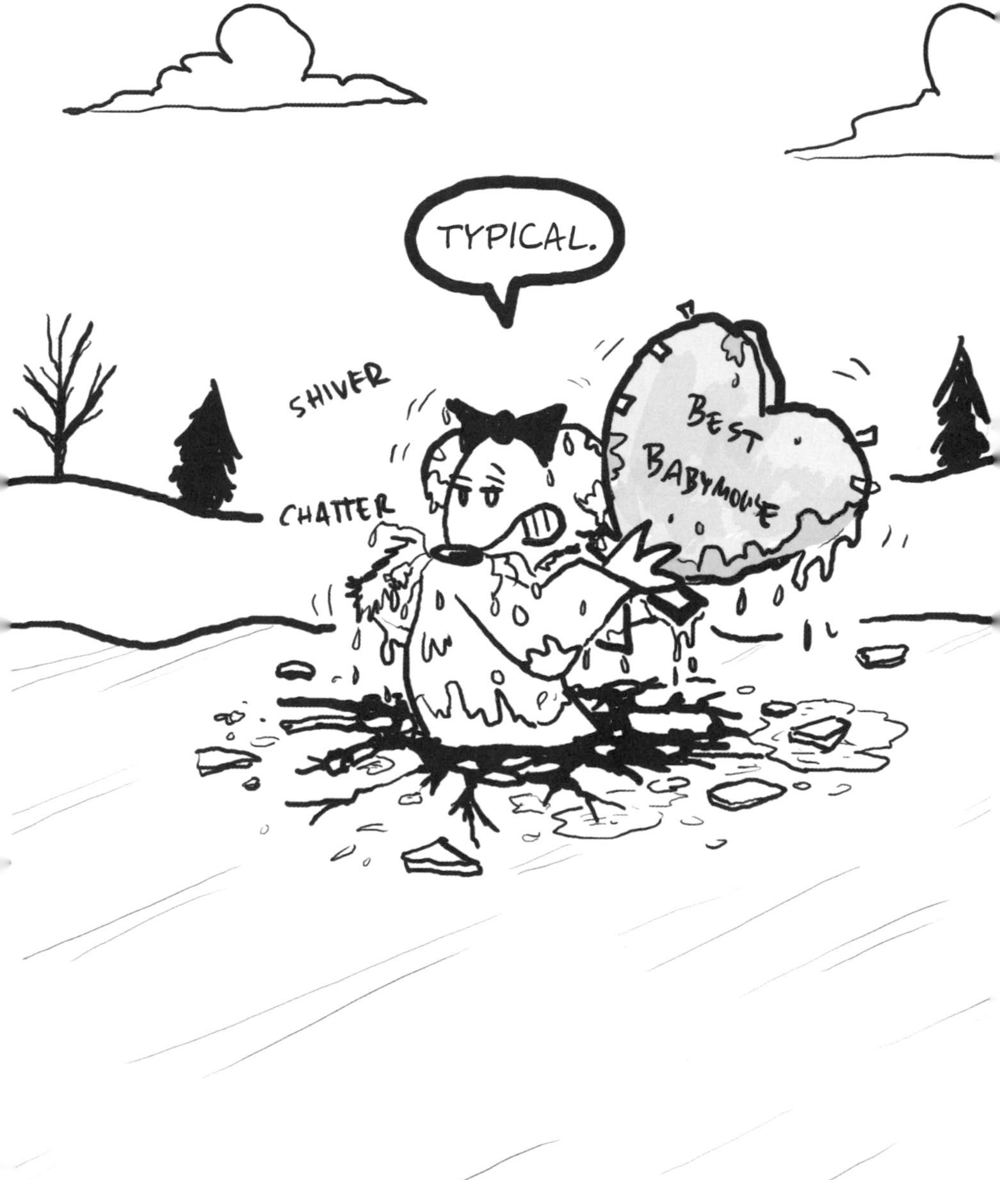
TYPICAL.
SHIVER
CHATTER
BEST BABYMOUSE

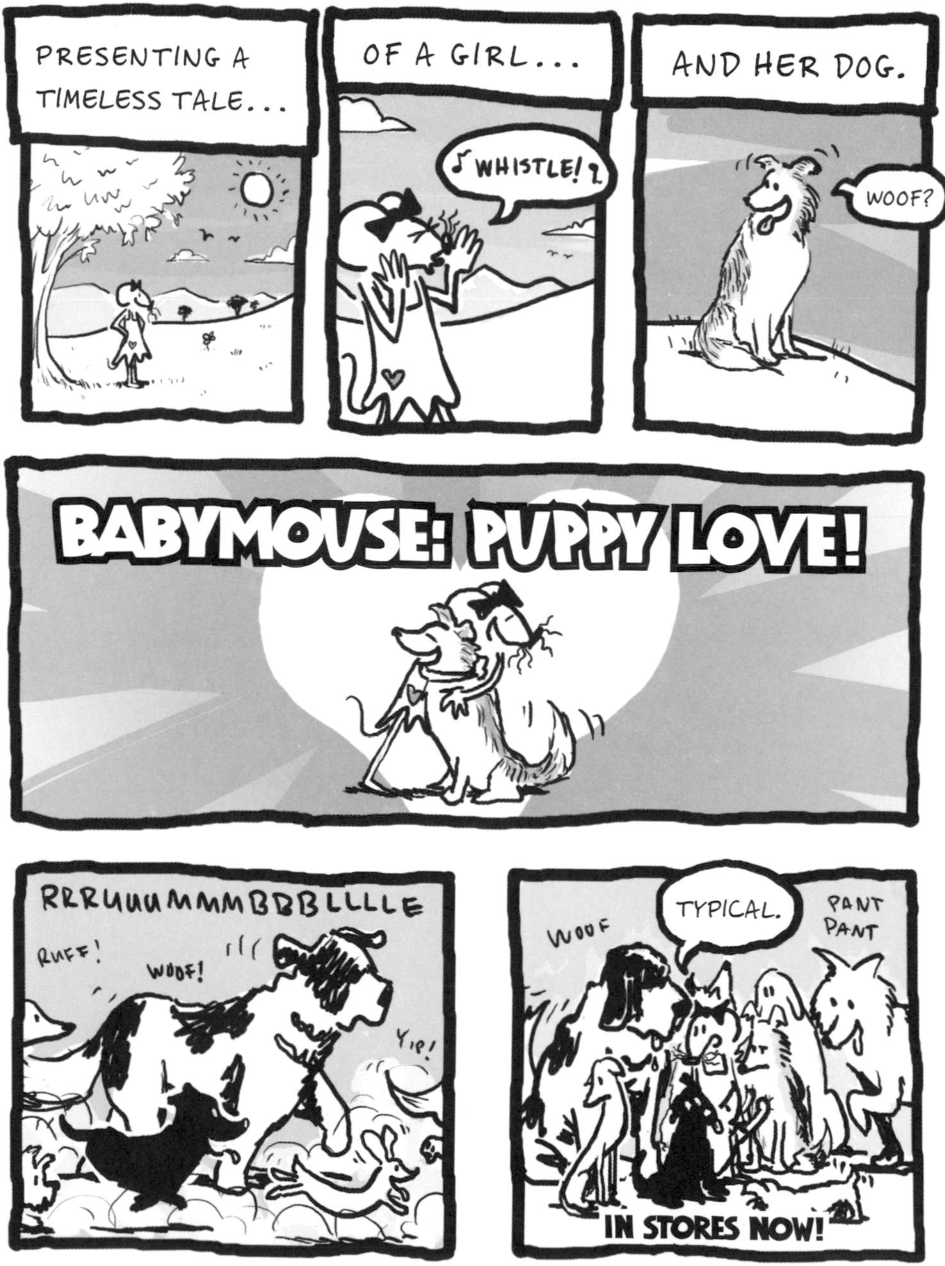
PRESENTING A TIMELESS TALE...
OF A GIRL...
WHISTLE!
AND HER DOG.
WOOF?
BABYMOUSE: PUPPY LOVE!
RRRUUUMMMMBBBLLLLE
RUFF!
WOOF!
YIP!
WOOF
TYPICAL.
PANT PANT
IN STORES NOW!